The Blood Secret

Revel Barker

P

Palatino Publishing

First published in 2013 by Palatino Publishing

By the same author:

The Hitler Scoop
Round Up The Usual Suspects (editor)
Field of Vision
Crying All The Way To The Bank: Liberace v. Cassandra and the Daily Mirror (Famous Trials)
The Mayor of Montebello

*Also available as E-books

ISBN: 978-1-907841-11-8

This book is a work of fiction. All the characters in it are fictitious and any resemblance to real persons, living or dead, is purely coincidental.

Palatino Publishing 66 Florence Road Brighton BN1 6DJ
United Kingdom
palatinobooks@gmail.com

Revel Barker was born and educated in Leeds. As a reporter his work appeared in every English national newspaper and in magazines including *Punch, The Oldie* and *Tribune*. He now lives in semi-retirement on an island in the Mediterranean.

This book is dedicated with love to
Anna, Angi, Julian and James
who came to the aid of the party

Part One
Prelude

The seven cardinals had arrived separately and ostensibly on foot. In fact they had each travelled from the Vatican by car, having given their drivers different instructions, and walked the last few hundred yards. Some of them had nominated churches as their supposed destinations; the two more energetic had been dropped off at the Pantheon and Piazza Navona, saying simply that they would walk from there, before winding their way through the ancient streets of religious institutions and clerical outfitters to via Monterone.

The beautifully frescoed early sixteenth-century Palazzo Lante della Rovere stood at number 85. Long before it became a restaurant the building had been the home of a Roman cardinal, a member of the Medici family, who was elected to the papacy as Leo X. Now the present-day cardinals used the unassuming entrance to the left of the more stately doorway before being led by a young African girl in colourful native costume to a heavy curtain behind which was the tall door of a private room.

There was absolutely no reason why any number of cardinals should not meet socially after attending an important conclave. But the city – like the Church – was a breeding ground of rumour, gossip and innuendo and they feared terms such as 'secrecy' and 'cabal'. The drivers were renowned for their discretion, but in a world that had too many conspiracy theorists for its own good it seemed that the best idea was to exercise extreme caution.

However, cardinals were not normally given to walking and usually insisted on being dropped right on the doorstep. When one of the men in the drivers' room mentioned that his passenger had got out of the car early, another six said that theirs had done the same. But they decided that, after being confined in a heated debate for two long days they might have felt the need for a stroll, even in the heavy evening air that was common to Rome, and the subject was never raised again.

Apart from the occasional grunt of approval or otherwise as they examined the French labels on wine bottles already opened in the centre of the table, nobody spoke until the last man arrived and took his seat. The cardinal who had convened the gathering was a tall angular man whose demeanour suggested he had seen it all, and had not been greatly impressed by any of it. He opened his hands to signal the start of conversation.

'Disaster,' said the first to speak.

'Calamity.'

'Catastrophe'... 'Debacle'... 'Tragedy'...

'A public relations shambles of seismic proportions...'

'At least John Paul – may his soul rest in peace – actually looked the part. But this fellow looks... well... creepy.'

'Nothing was more predictable than that the main

gist of the news would be that we had elected a former member of the Hitler Youth. It makes no difference that every German youngster was expected to join it, nor even that his parents were said to be opposed to the Nazis. The simple fact is that the most newsworthy element was that he had been a member.'

'The kindest nickname anybody came up with was Papa Ratzi...'

'Linking him with the photographers who were blamed for the death of Princess Diana...'

'And then inevitably it became Papa Nazi.'

'The German Shepherd was okay, except it's a dog...'

'Better, anyway, than Cardinal Rottweiler.'

'Throw in the information that he has a long record for defending abusive priests, plus of course that he was in charge of the Congregation of the Doctrine of the Faith – which everybody still thinks of as the Inquisition – and... it's a fiasco.'

'You even need to wonder what John Paul was thinking of, as a Pole, when he appointed a German as the prefect of what was historically essentially an anti-Jewish department.'

'A German Pope. That says it all.'

'It is done, now. There is nothing we can do to change it.'

'Unless he resigns.'

'The Holy Father does not resign.'

'But, after a decent interval, if he is prevented from doing any more damage for a short number of years, he might be persuaded to retire, on the grounds of ill-health. It would be an acceptable excuse.'

What had further angered the Italian cardinals was that in the first ballot their own favoured candidate, Carlo Maria Martini, Archbishop of Milan, had received the most votes. Ratzinger, the German, had been placed second but it was thought that, because he was also presiding over the election as Dean of the College of Cardinals, he would not be considered an appropriate contender. There had also been a small number of votes for the Third World candidate, Cardinal Bergoglio, Archbishop of Buenos Aires.

But in the second ballot Ratzinger's votes had actually increased, and in the third he polled sixty-five, against Bergoglio's thirty-five. With 115 cardinals attending and voting, and seventy-seven votes theoretically required for an outright winner, it seemed unnecessary to continue with the election. Ratzinger, as president, asked for a unanimous vote to secure his position. He received 107 of the 115, following which white smoke was emitted from the chimney of the Sistine Chapel to announce to the thousands of faithful who filled St Peter's Square *Habemus Papam*: 'We have a Pope'.

The cardinals fell silent as missionary sisters knocked on the door and entered with the first course, scallops on spinach in flaky pastry with white wine and cream.

'It is not as if it's the first time, even in very recent history,' said the convenor when the door was closed again. 'Albino Luciani was a mistake. He lasted only thirty-three days but it did irreparable damage to the Mother Church.'

Luciani, who became John Paul I in 1978, died mysteriously amid rumours that he had either been poisoned – because he was about to expose fraud inside the freemasonry of the Vatican Bank – or given no help when he suffered a stroke because he had suggested a number of sweeping reforms including reversal of the Church's ban on contraception. The Curia had refused to allow an autopsy and it was claimed by some insiders that, after dying in a corridor, his body had been placed in his bed, his spectacles put on his head and a book propped in his hand so that when found 'officially' he would appear to have died peacefully while reading.

'History is always repeating itself. Go back far enough and it is recorded that there was a plot to poison the very Pope who built the house in which we are currently dining.'

The cardinals fell silent, remembering both the circumstances and the history. There was no point in debating those matters further, now.

The waitresses – missionary nuns from around the world who operated the restaurant as a charity called *l'Eau Vive* – returned to collect the empty plates and replace them with fillet of beef in horseradish sauce with dauphine potatoes, the convenor taking the opportunity to remind his fellow diners that the restaurant offered a generous discount of twelve per cent to members of the clergy. He added, pointedly, that the takings – including staff gratuities – all went to the missionary charity, so the 'discount' could become a tip.

As the door closed again, one of the cardinals said: 'So name me a perfect Pope.... not John Paul II, the Pole, canonising more saints than the total of his predecessors in the previous five centuries, and jetting around the world collecting air miles on Alitalia flights. One hundred and twenty-nine different countries...'

'He was trying to draw attention to world poverty, surely a good thing,' interjected one of the cardinals who – like all of the men sitting around the table – had actually been elevated by 'the Pole'.

'If you want to highlight the poverty on this earth there are better ways of doing it than shipping out your personal armour-plated vehicle and appearing in front of the masses accompanied by fat bishops.'

'And he was a great promoter of world peace, even to the extent of advocating what he described as a new religious armada with an alliance involving Jews and Protestants.... We are all under daily attack by the Moslems.'

'Yes, and he might have done it, had he lived longer. Certainly some form of reconciliation with the Jews, at least. Because, like every Pope before him, he knew The Blood Secret. He actually made a start, but his time was running out. So what he should have done was clearly nominate his successor and prepare him for it. Ratzinger knew the Secret, even before his election. The question is whether he does anything about it. He won't, because he's a German. And that, my dear brethren, could be his downfall... And worse, far worse, it could become the beginning of ours.'

'Ours?'

'The entire Holy Mother Church.'

The convenor said he could highly recommend *Coupe Galilee* – vanilla ice cream with figs, tangerine and liqueur – for dessert.

When the meal was over and cognac was being served he put a cigarette in his mouth and, in response to a disapproving look from the man beside him, said quietly: 'Non-smoking is upstairs, on the *piano nobile,* where the frescoes are.'

Next time the door was opened the cardinals could hear the sisters' nightly singing of *Ave Maria of Lourdes* to the customers, mainly tourists, in the public area.

When it closed again the cardinal at the end of the table, a man almost as wide as he was tall with a tonsured head like a crimson bowling ball who was still smarting over the reference to fat bishops, asked: 'Forgive me, but am I the only person here who is not privy to this Blood Secret?'

One
L-Erbgha

There were only two passengers in business class on the morning Air Malta flight out of Heathrow. One had a mop of dark brown hair and was in his forties, tall and lean and pale, but looking as if he might spend a bit of time in a gym; the other was over sixty, around medium height, pink-faced and chubby with a shock of pure white hair and looking as if he never ventured far from a restaurant table. But they both wore lightweight tweed jackets and stone-coloured trousers with deck shoes, identifying them as Brits following the smart-casual dress code, so they nodded to each other as they threw their wheelie bags into the overhead lockers at opposite sides of the aisle.

The taller man strapped himself in and took a copy of *Private Eye* from his jacket pocket. His travelling companion extracted a *Daily Telegraph* from a pouch on the side of his travelling bag and snapped the locker shut. He dropped his jacket onto the empty seat beside him and made himself comfortable while rather clumsily folding the broadsheet newspaper into four to expose the crossword puzzle. Then he fastened his seatbelt, took a ballpoint pen from his shirt pocket, and commenced filling in squares.

The aircraft was still taxiing towards take-off when he waved the newspaper across the aisle and smiled and said: '*Telegraph*? I only take it for the crossword.'

'Thanks... *Private Eye*?'

'No, *grazie*. Read it in the common room.'

The young man held the newspaper full out, then folded it into three, lengthways, so he could read down the columns, a knack he had perfected through travelling to work in crowded tube trains. He only scanned the pages; most of it he had seen on TV the previous day, which he considered both the curse and the blessing of twenty-hour news channels.

Passing it back he thanked the man and asked: 'Holiday?'

'No. Live there. You?'

'Business.'

'Computers? That's basically the only business nowadays, apart, of course, from the distribution and opening of brown envelopes. Something connected with the government, is it?'

'Not exactly. I'm a police officer. Got an investigation. Dead Brit. Suspicious circumstances.' He didn't know who he was talking to so he changed the subject.

'How long have you lived there?'

'Off and on, all my life... so far. I was born in Malta. Father in the Royal Marines. I went to UK for school and university, and stayed there to work, term-time, but this has always been home base.'

'What's it like... Malta?'

The man grinned. 'What have you heard about it?'

'Oh... sunshine resort... friendly folk... very pro-Brit. That sort of thing.'

The older man smiled broadly. 'Well, it's a resort destination with hardly any beaches. Half the people are friendly, and half are probably pro-Brit. Not necessarily the same people in the same halves. Some of them have never forgiven the UK for answering their plea to kick the Frogs out in 1800. Some of them are still moaning that if they hadn't been occupied by us they wouldn't have been bombed in World War Two. Half of them – not necessary the same half as the other halves – hark back to their occupation by the Knights as the glory days. But the Knights treated them as slaves, and wouldn't let them join the Order because, probably rightly, they didn't recognise what the Maltese called their nobility; their baronetage had more to do with land ownership than family lineage. The result is that they venerate the Knights' cross, which is on their coins, their buildings, and everywhere else, and resent the George Cross being on their flag. Yet when Napoleon turned up in Grand Harbour, the Knights ran off and left them to it. So they came to the Royal Navy to free them from the Frog.'

He was getting into his stride, now.

'We gave them the vote before the War and then their independence in 1964 during the Great British Empire closing-down sale. They weren't ready for it. It was like your kid saying he wants a motorbike, but he doesn't want driving lessons and he won't need a crash helmet but you buy him a bike anyway and leave him to it. Now he thinks he's a world-class racer, but he has still to learn to maintain his balance.

'We supported the bloody place for 264 years, and we're still supporting it. First, after independence, we paid for the shipyards, and they wrecked them. Now our taxes – along with the Frogs and the Krauts – are paying for eighty-five per cent of everything they spend. They resent that, too. But they take the money of course.'

His diatribe was interrupted by the flight attendant offering them complimentary drinks. The man sipped at his gin and tonic and continued:

'Pro-Brit, you think? We are charged more than the locals for travelling on their buses and there's a different rate for all foreigners for essentials such as electricity and water. If you want to bring a car from overseas Maltese registration will cost something equivalent to the value of the vehicle. We have to pay for hospital treatment – even in the hospitals we built for them.'

Tourism, he said, was the islands' biggest industry by far; but the Maltese didn't understand it...

'They rip off tourists on the basis that they are not likely to return, so they might as well get the money while they're here. They don't realise that the main reason they won't return is that they keep getting ripped off.'

He sighed. 'They're totally disorganised, lacking the basics like logic, courtesy and common sense. They are still using carbon paper and yet they think they're the centre of the IT world. They fancied themselves as off-shore bankers, but they take thirty days to clear a foreign cheque. The kids can't do their ten-times table without a calculator, they speak no known language, and they think they are cultured Romans. But the truth is that they're a bloody rabble. They're basically Arabs.'

The man was clearly on his hobby horse.

'It's the same with government. Fifty per cent nationalist and fifty per cent labour. Elections are a farce. All that changes is the names on the brown envelopes for back-handers. And with religion. Ninety-six per cent Roman Catholic, they say. Half could tell you the Ten Commandments and cite the seven deadly sins, and the others see them as a challenge. Adultery, for example, is a national pastime, more popular than football. Brothel-keeping is the only trade they've ever been any good at. Half are bent as paper clips and the other half are lawyers, that's not to suggest that some or most of the lawyers aren't also bent, because...'

He raised his shoulders, and shrugged, without finishing his point.

'Because they're not necessarily the same fifty per cent... So why do you still live in Malta?'

'I don't. I live on Gozo. Different place, different race. Even different lace. Certainly a different face.' He appeared to be pleased with the rhyming, and beamed contentedly.

'In fact an artist or sculptor would tell you there are fewer than ten differing facial features on Gozo. All in-bred, you see. Half of them never left the island and the half that did went to Melbourne or New York for work and miraculously found and married somebody with roots in the same village. The four-mile channel between the two islands is what separates Europe from north Africa. That's the truth of it.'

'How is Gozo different?'

'Greener, cleaner, quieter. The people are more secretive – that's the Sicilian inheritance – but they are fine with tourists, except for the Maltese who use the place as a weekend retreat. They never lock their cars and they leave their keys in the front door... except at weekends and in August, when the Maltese cross over. They don't like the Malts, and the feeling is mutual. The Maltese treat them like we supposedly see the Irish – as ill-educated and unsophisticated country bumpkins. They're laid back, all right, virtually horizontal. But they are like the Irish in that they don't take themselves too seriously. It's all to do with having a different history. Gozo was depopulated at least twice, and refilled by Sicilians.'

The young man raised the arm of his seat so he could slide nearer to the aisle to listen and learn more. And in what was left of the three-hour flight he learnt what was obviously almost the entire history of the Maltese archipelago along with a description of local society from ineffectual magistrates to abusive priests; from the number of public holidays – 'they usually spend four days celebrating the memory of St Joseph the Worker, but there's no concept here of irony' – to the illegal shooting and trapping of migrating birds.

It soon dawned on him that, for all his harsh

criticism of its perversities and inadequacies, the fellow loved – or was at least inordinately fond of – the islands, both Malta and Gozo. He was merely exercising the traditional English right to carp about that which he was most closely connected to.

He laughed a lot as he spoke, and when he wasn't laughing maintained a cherubic smile. Occasionally he winked, as if signalling that he was being ironic. His one-man audience thought he looked like a clean-shaven out-of-season Santa Claus.

So he heard about the occupation by Phoenicians and Carthaginians (800-218 BC), The Romans and the Byzantines (218 BC - AD 870), the Arabs (870-1091), the Normans, the Swabians and the Angevins, (1091-1282) 'starting with Roger the Norman, King of Sicily – and what language, one wonders, did he speak?', the Spanish (1282-1530), the Knights of St John (1530-1798) and the French (1798-1800).

'I apologise.... occupational hazard... thirty years of teaching history and I guess it's difficult to stop. Especially with a captive audience.'

'No... it's fine. History was always my favourite subject.' He only wished his teachers had been as easy-going and as erudite as the guy sitting across the aisle.

But had he heard, for example, about the Siege of Malta (1565)?

'Of course you haven't, because it isn't taught in history in mainland Europe. Yet Elizabeth the First had said it was the single factor that stopped the entire continent becoming Moslem...'

As they flew over the north coast of Gozo, losing

height in preparation for landing at Luqa, the man ended his lecture.

'It's a fascinating history, for such a tiny island.'

'Yes... but the important thing is that it's the history of the islands, not the history of the Maltese. The population doesn't actually figure much in it.... Anyway, tell me... your dead Brit...?'

'John McAuliffe, businessman...'

'Johnny Cash, they call him, here. Now, there's a man who knows his brown envelopes, both giving and receiving.'

'You know... knew... him?'

'Not personally. But he's a well-known Mr Fixit. Or should I say he was? I hadn't heard he was dead.'

'Day before yesterday. The local boys have some doubt about the manner of his death, but it's probably all pretty routine. Probably cut and dried by now. Straight in and out, for me...'

'Well, if you're still here at the weekend, come over to Gozo on Saturday. It's open house, and you can see for yourself the difference in the two islands.'

After a pause he said: 'Anyway, the cops in Malta don't work weekends, except those working on traffic, so there'll be nothing for you to do.'

He took a wallet from the breast pocket of his shirt and extracted a business card. It bore the Oxford University crest and said he was Emeritus Professor Duncan Ashe.

'Duncan...? Bob...' the two men shook hands.

As the Boeing landed they heard the passengers in economy class clapping... 'See what I mean about how bloody primitive they are?'

He shook his head as if in disbelief at what he was seeing and hearing: 'I'm surprised they don't go round with a hat and take a collection for the driver.'

On the aircraft steps the heat hit Bob so fiercely that he felt as if his trousers were being ironed while he was wearing them. They were directed onto a coach for the fifty-yard journey to passport control.

'See what I mean?' he asked again. 'Somebody's brother-in-law has the airport coach concession, I'll wager. Welcome to Malta!'

Neither of them had any hold luggage so they walked together through passport control down the escalator and through uninterested Customs into the arrivals hall. People in the waiting crowd held pieces of paper with names scrawled on them.

Bob pointed towards a man in a green polo shirt and blue slacks.

'Er... this is for me...'

'Bob *Shilling*...?'

'Real name's David. But I've been Bob since junior school. Obvious reasons.'

'I'm desperate for a fag... You a smoker? There's a place you can have a cigarette and a half-decent cup of coffee. You'll not be able to smoke in the cop car. Nor anywhere else.'

'You can smoke in the car,' the man with the name-card told him while making a faint nod in Ashe's direction: acknowledging a distant acquaintance rather than a friendship.

Shilling gave him the once-over: sunglasses on top of black wavy hair, Roman nose, a full but closely cropped moustache, his face creased into what appeared to be a permanent smile. You'll do, he thought.

To Ashe he said:

'Then I'd better be off. Sooner I get started, the sooner I finish, I guess.'

They shook hands again and the professor, cigarette packet in his hand, headed to the coffee bar, telling him not to forget Gozo, Saturday, and Shilling walked over to the waiting car, its hazard lights flashing on double yellow lines outside the terminal building.

Two

During the fifteen-minute car journey to police headquarters Shilling had opened the sky-blue folder that had been left on the front passenger seat and started to read.

'I've never heard of anybody being killed by a broken finger,' he said.

Senior inspector Jesmond Galea, negotiating a massive roundabout with five lanes of traffic, none of them giving way, thought to himself that this was typical of fast-track officers; they tended to read the beginning of a report and comment on it before they'd digested all the facts.

'Read the rest of it.'

The autopsy had revealed a small contusion on the skull, causing a bruise on the brain. The victim's arms showed signs of having been tied or strapped down, probably to the arms of a chair. These were the marks that had elevated the case from a probably interrupted burglary to a homicide.

'If you are 83,' said Galea, 'and you have a weak heart, and you are tied to a chair, and your finger is broken... well, you might think the heart might give out. Which makes it murder.'

'What were the burglars after?'

'Don't know. So far as we can establish, nothing is missing. But if you're robbing a house and the owner comes in and surprises you, and you tie him up and he dies, you might decide to make your getaway empty-handed, I suppose. After all, if you were caught with the goods it would immediately implicate you in the death... But the interesting thing...'

'But why would you break his finger?'

'Maybe to shut him up. Perhaps he was shouting.'

'Why wouldn't they just gag him? That would have been easier. You wouldn't break somebody's finger to keep him quiet, would you?'

'Don't know. But he wasn't gagged when we found him.'

Malta police headquarters were in Floriana, just outside the capital city, Valletta, in a building that had once been the actual hospital for the 'Hospitaller' Knights of St John. Galea led Shilling along the corridors of the third floor where CID was based and sent a clerk to tell the superintendent that their guest had arrived from London.

'You've interviewed the widow?'

She had found the body, and reported the death to the police. In Shilling's experience the person who 'found' the body was the most likely prime suspect in a murder case, and the spouse usually came a close second.

'Of course. At the estimated time of the death she was playing bridge with friends. So there are three witnesses to support her alibi.'

Bugger. So they could rule her out. 'You interviewed the other bridge players?'

'No. But she'd hardly have named them, unless they were going to agree with what she said. I mean, would she? Anyway, the really interesting thing is that...'

Galea was interrupted by the arrival of his superintendent, a big man with a heavyweight boxer's physique and gait and a totally bald head, the sort of hairlessness that looked as though it might have been caused by an illness, removing the hair from even eyebrows and eyelids.

He greeted Shilling and then immediately asked him to send his greetings to a number of top-ranking officers at the Yard who he had met at various Interpol seminars. Obviously trying to impress his subordinates.

Shilling, who had carried out investigations in France, Germany, Canada and Austria, had never attended any meeting of Interpol.

To the superintendent, the case seemed fairly simple. A burglary attempt – for it was well known that John McAuliffe was a very wealthy man – interrupted by the houseowner who was then tied up, bringing on a heart attack. 'He dies, so they make themselves scarce, pretty damn quick. You don't want to hang about when there's a corpse on the scene of a robbery.'

'I ought to see the body. And I'd like a word with the widow.'

'Of course. Tomorrow for all that. We have booked you in, here, for the night, and a few of us thought we could have dinner tonight. Give you chance to acclimatise. Inspector Galea will obviously need to get back home, but we can fill you in on the background to friend McAuliffe over a decent meal.'

'I could maybe have a look at the body in the meantime. Get that over with...'

'Tomorrow. Dump your stuff, have a wander round the city. Relax. Enjoy it. We'll pick you up around eight.'

Galea drove him the few hundred yards to the Phoenicia Hotel. 'You were going to say something you thought was interesting...'

'You think the body is here, in Malta, don't you? It isn't. It's on Gozo. That's where he died, or was killed.'

'The reports I read said it was in Malta.'

'Yes. But Gozo is in Malta. And that's not the interesting thing. The interesting thing is that there were two burglaries. One on Malta, the other on Gozo. McAuliffe had houses on both islands. They spent most of the summer on Gozo, and the Malta house was broken into while they were there, probably on the same day.'

'And the widow?'

'She's back here. Birgu. That's Malta. Well... she didn't want to stay in the house where she found the body, I guess. So you can see her in the morning, before we go to Gozo. Then you can see the body in the morgue, and see where we go from there... Me... I'll come over in the morning to pick you up and take you to meet her.'

Shilling checked in to his hotel, dropped his bag in the room, briefly studied the view from his balcony of part of Malta's famous Grand Harbour, and walked out again into brilliant hot sunshine. The five-star former Grand Tour hotel was on the peninsular on which the knights had built the renaissance city of Valletta – 'a city built by gentlemen, for gentlemen', Ashe had said, quoting Benjamin Disraeli.

With single-deck coaches spewing exhaust fumes and coming at speed in all directions he carefully picked his way through the main bus terminal to the far side of the promontory and found himself looking down on the southern side of the harbour and the original Three Cities where the Knights had made their heroic last stand against the Turks in 1565 – right up to the moment when the relief forces arrived like the Seventh Cavalry and drove the invaders back to their ships and away from the islands for ever. During the siege the Turks had rained shells down on the three harbour cities from where he was standing. It was called Mount Sciberras in those days. Grand Master Jean de la Valette – so exhausted by the battle that he had to sit, sword in hand, in an armchair to await what he expected to be the final Turkish onslaught – had eventually learnt the lesson of holding the high ground, and immediately started building a new hilltop headquarters for the Order, as the city that would bear his name.

Impressed by the amount of local history he realised he already knew, Shilling walked back between the careering coaches to the City Gate. Less impressive than its name, he thought. Almost reminiscent of East Berlin in its plain, drab concrete sunlit simplicity.

Inside the Gate he was surprised to find the usual

tourist tat – the 'kiss-me-quick' style of souvenir that he'd expect in Blackpool or Southend but not, somehow, in a city that was famous for its style and architecture. He ignored the tea towels, flimsy T-shirts and henna tattoos, the obviously machine-made 'Maltese lace' and the primitive prints of local fishing boats. In the searing heat he needed a hat. The hawker, recognising a tourist, asked for fifteen euros and eventually settled for five, then offered Shilling sunglasses and flick-knives, all at 'special prices for my English friend'.

He looked briefly at the ruins of the Royal Opera House, bombed during the Second World War and still a bomb site in spite of donations for its rebuilding from the Germans (who had flattened it) and the British (who had been held responsible). That money – Ashe had told him – was almost certainly in some former minister's Swiss bank account.

He was in Republic Street, built by the Knights as Strada Royale, renamed Kingsway by the Brits, and then named again as a defiant gesture of independence. He was impressed to realise that he was walking the streets where the Knights, descendants of the Crusaders, had trodden, and could admire the architecture that they had bequeathed. It was just a pity, he thought, that the town planners had permitted swinging shop signs and garish facades on shops, down the ages. He found a coffee bar, ordered a cappuccino, and sat beneath an umbrella, his feet suddenly surrounded by pigeons, but otherwise alone with his thoughts.

Two robberies, one murder. Did that mean two teams, working in concert, or one team, working consecutively on different islands? When McAuliffe died, did the Gozo team phone Malta and tell them to call it all off and make themselves scarce?

Two burglaries, but nothing stolen... How unusual, and how unlikely, was that?

Or... was it simply nothing stolen that had yet been missed?

He kicked the pigeons away, but they moved only slightly, then waddled back. Other customers, tourists and locals, were dropping food for them from their tables. Great, he thought. They had made it illegal to feed pigeons in Trafalgar Square and the birds had quickly vanished. Here, they fed them and the ancient stone-paved square was covered in bird shit. He purposely dropped his lighted cigarette end on the ground. One of the birds picked it up in its beak by the filter tip and, with a single jerk of its supple neck, contemptuously tossed it away.

He walked back to the Phoenicia, pausing in front of a statue of Jean Parisot de la Valette. If you could see your city now, he thought. The beautiful architecture is still here, but it's been ruined by the developers. You should never have left it to the Maltese... He was beginning to think like Ashe, he thought.

Dinner, with five senior police officers, was in a restaurant down a set of stairs and decorated with what were probably portraits of its best customers in a bygone era. They all ordered the same food – foie gras as a starter, followed by Irish rib-eye – so, assuming that they would know the menu, and the chef, he opted for the same thing.

He didn't learn much from the conversation, except that, having been founded in 1814, the Maltese Police Force pre-dated the Met by fifteen years... and that they had all known John McAuliffe, and seemed to think that he was a bit of a character and an all-round good guy..

'He was on our radar at the Yard,' Shilling told them, 'because he was dealing in arms, from Libya to Ireland, for example.'

'He was an authorised arms dealer,' said one of them. 'He could sell guns and ammunition to anywhere he wanted, provided he had a licence.'

'But not to the bloody IRA, though. And not to other terrorist factions in Europe.'

'If it's true that he did that... well... we can assure you that none of the stuff actually passed through, was actually landed in, Malta. So it wouldn't be any concern of ours.'

'No...? He just ran the operation from Malta... so you weren't bothered about that?'

'A lot of our entrepreneurs do business with Libya. We are a neutral nation. We don't take sides. We also keep our links with Libya open, which in the long term has to be a benefit for the rest of Europe.'

'So if the stuff isn't actually landed in Malta, if it doesn't physically come off the plane or through Customs, it's of no interest to you, is it? It can fly via Malta – how else would it get out of Libya? – but if it doesn't touch Maltese soil you don't care what it is or where it's going?'

'No... Why would we? Why should we? Johnny McAuliffe had a legitimate business. He dealt in arms, totally legally. And he ran security for several governments, especially from north Africa, around Europe. It brings money to Malta, in the long term. As we say, it was legitimate business.'

On an archipelago that might see half a dozen murders in a bad year, there was no call for a specialist homicide division; when a serious crime occurred it would fall to whichever senior officer was available to oversee it, usually from a distance. The bald officer who Shilling had met first and appeared from the deference shown by the other diners to be the most senior man at the table had been mainly silent while his colleagues answered Shilling's questions.

After what might have been a thoughtful silence he told him:

'You've got a foreign assignment. Good for you. But it's a straightforward killing, virtually an accidental death, not a planned murder. So please don't try to turn this into some sort of international incident, just to justify your air fare and hotel expenses.'

'The death may not have been premeditated. We don't know. But it's still murder in the furtherance of theft. That used to be a capital offence.'

'So did adultery, if you go back far enough.' The superintendent's colleagues all laughed at that comment.

'But it's today's news and tomorrow's history. It'll be forgotten as soon as the funeral is over.'

Shilling told the men that the distance back to his hotel was short enough for him to walk. He noticed that the waiter didn't bring them a bill.

Three

Il-Hamis

The route from his hotel to the McAuliffe's' main Malta residence loosely followed the waterfront of Grand Harbour, past the wharves, quays, docks and boatyards to Birgu, and a former Knight's palace separated from the water only by the width of a road. Shilling realised that he had been gazing down on the building's facade from his vantage point in Valletta the previous afternoon. Thanks to his new knowledge of history he could date it fairly accurately – between 1530, when the knights arrived on the island and occupied what were known as the Three Cities of the harbour, and 1566, when they all relocated to the new city of Valletta.

During the journey he had examined the personal effects of the dead man that Inspector Galea was returning to the widow in a manila envelope so large it belied the size of its contents: one blue handkerchief, one gold ('yellow metal', it said on the outside of the package) Rolex Oyster wristwatch, one key-chain with four keys on a ring, one pocket diary, one slim black leather crocodile pattern belt.

Shilling weighed the watch in his hand.

'Bit old-fashioned, but cost a fortune when it was new. Still worth two or three grand of anybody's money.'

'He was in his eighties. He was a bit old fashioned, himself.'

'The keys?'

'One for each house. One for his office.'

'The fourth one – the Chubb? Could be for a safe?

'Don't know. Presumably the widow will tell us.'

Shilling flicked through the pages of the diary, which showed a complete week, Monday to Sunday, on each double-page spread.

'He had his own code, or shorthand... *TF, TT* and *A*... what do we think that means? And here, on his last day, the day he was killed: *TF Vatman 8*... What's that?'

'Don't know,' said Galea. 'Maybe the widow can tell us.'

There were a number of cars parked directly outside the house and across the road, on the water side, was a metallic silver Ford Escort with a man sitting alone in it.

'You have somebody watching the house?'

'No.'

'So what's Chummy doing, over there?'

'It's a rental car. Maybe he's somebody's driver.'

'Let's go and ask him.'

But when they walked towards the car it was suddenly started and driven off. As it passed the two policemen Shilling noticed the Avis sticker on the rear windscreen. 'How could you tell, from the distance we were at, that it was a rental?'

'The registration: three letters... if the third one is K it's a hire car. It helps us keep an eye on insurance, roadworthiness, and tax. In theory it also warns locals that the driver is probably foreign and may have difficulty in finding his way around and be deserving of a little extra courtesy and tolerance.' He paused and added: 'As if...'

They rapped on the door using an iron knocker in the shape of a Knights cross. One of the huge imposing oak double doors was opened by the maid, who Galea introduced to Shilling as Concetta, the woman who had reported the break-in at the house. She led the officers through a huge vaulted entrance hall to a high-ceilinged drawing room with oil paintings on panelled walls, and green leather armchairs and sofas, where the widow McAuliffe sat alone at an antique writing table.

Shilling shook her hand, rather self-consciously saying 'I am sorry for your loss.' It was something he said often, and he always thought it sounded trite. But he didn't know what else you were supposed to say to the bereaved.

The widow was a slim striking looking woman with shoulder length hair the colour of a new penny; even sitting down it was clear that she was tall for a Maltese. She looked at her watch, appeared to sigh at the time it showed, then told Concetta to bring coffee and gestured for the men to draw armchairs up to the other side of the table.

She asked Galea whether he had any news for her. He said he hadn't, but that his colleague may have a few extra questions that might help their inquiry.

'Did you or your husband have any visitors on the day he died?' – No.

Galea had told him he had already asked the question; he had also made the routine format enquiries about whether the victim had any known enemies, or any particular worries. The answer to all of them was still negative, but Shilling liked to see for himself how the interviewee answered the questions; the vocal tone and body language could sometimes be as important as the actual oral responses.

'Did either of you receive any telephone calls that day?'

The phone was always ringing, she said. Her husband had never retired. He was still doing business. They had an arrangement so that any call to the Birgu house would be rerouted automatically to the Xaghra house.

Shilling, notepad on his knee, was writing *Sharra* when Galea leaned across and spelt out the village name for him. The two Maltese smiled at each other, and at the ignorance of an Englishman.

'Any unusual calls?'

'I wouldn't know. He usually noted the important ones in his diary...' She opened it at random. *TF*, that's incoming, it means Telephone From... *TT* is calls he made: Telephone To.'

As simple as that.

'And the capital *A*...?' Shilling leaned across the table and placed his forefinger on one of the entries.

'That's not an *A*; it's a pair of dividers, or a compass. Those are various lodge meetings. Weekly meetings and business meetings.... '

'No unusual or unexpected calls, though?'

'I don't think so. But this...' she had turned to the last completed page.

'*Vatman 8*. I don't know what that might be.'

'His accountant, maybe? The person who deals with his VAT returns, perhaps? Or perhaps the tax office?'

'No, look...' she flipped back a few pages. 'The accountant is here... Franco. And the VAT office wouldn't ring John directly, they would deal with Franco.'

She looked at her wristwatch and shook it, as though with exasperation. 'What time is it?'

'Five-past nine,' Galea told her. She sighed again. Then Shilling asked whether he could see where the break-in had occurred.

He followed Concetta through the large house – it was indeed a palace, albeit a small one – to French windows overlooking the garden. She showed him a shiny new pane of glass, replacing the one that had been broken to facilitate entry. She had called the glazier and had it replaced after SOCO, the Scene of Crime officers, had examined it for fingerprints. There was a good-sized garden, with rose bushes, at the back of the house. Its high walls would have afforded privacy to any burglar and the doors themselves would have been no obstacle once a pane was broken to allow him to reach through to the primitive lever locking mechanism.

Back in the drawing room, Shilling stood and looked at the paintings. He knew nothing about art, but the oils on the walls looked old and valuable. There were no empty spaces, no spare hooks.

'They were not after the paintings?'

'Not after them, no. But they removed most of

them from the wall. When I came in, most of them had been taken down from the walls and were on the floor.'

'Fingerprints?' Concetta had not been able to remove all traces of the very fine powder used for taking prints.

'There were fingerprints, yes,' said Galea. 'But none that meant anything to us. Nobody known.'

'Looking for a safe, then.'

'If they were, they didn't find it,' Mrs McAuliffe told him.

Shilling picked up the keys and gestured with the Chubb. 'This?'

'Yes; that's John's safe key.'

'And the safe...?'

'It's behind the bookcase.'

You could usually tell the difference between a Maltese property and a foreigner's home, Ashe had told him, because most Maltese wouldn't possess a bookcase. But John McAuliffe was an Englishman; he would buy and read books.

Shilling looked at the vast, cumbersome piece of furniture. Possibly Victorian. He scanned the shelves; some of the volumes were bound in sombre black, imprinted with sharp white titling, and were about the history of Malta, but chiefly about the Knights. The rest had mainly drab coloured spines: heavy subjects, heavy reading, heavy bookcase.

'How on earth do you...'

'Oh... it's on rollers. Push it... slide it to the left towards the door...'

Belying its weight the bulky bookcase slid, glided,

along the wall, revealing the grey door of a large built-in safe.

'Do you know what's in it?'

'I have no idea. Money, share certificates and so on, I expect. And my jewellery. Here's the key. Take a look.'

There were four shelves, including the bottom of the safe. One of them was stacked with packs of fifty and hundred euro banknotes. One of them had filing folders containing share certificates and what looked like ledgers and business documents, one a jewellery box containing pearl and diamond necklaces, ornamental rings, and earrings. On the shallow top shelf was a picture frame that Shilling extracted to look at.

It was a black and white print of a knight of Malta, obviously of very high rank, with the eight-pointed Knights' cross on the breastplate of his silver-metalled armour. He had a large square jaw, swollen like half a bag of sugar, a long prominent nose and a pot belly.

'Do we know who this is?' He handed it to the widow who glanced at it only briefly and then threw it furiously across the room towards a waste-paper basket, audibly cracking the glass.

'Hompesch!' she said. 'A traitor to Malta!'

She called Concetta. 'Take that out, and put it with the rubbish! Hompesch, indeed! Why in God's name would he have kept that? Why in the safe? It's a mystery to me.'

Shilling asked her whether he could take away some of the business files, to read later, in case they provided any clues and the woman said that yes; of course, he could take anything he wanted.

'We'll leave you with the key... and the money. There'll be a matter of probate, at some time, but meanwhile...'

'Meanwhile,' continued Galea, 'we haven't counted the money. We don't know how much is there. That is not our concern.'

Neither of the detectives could think of anything else to ask.

Shilling stood, this time preparatory to leaving. 'We will get these documents and ledgers back to you as quickly as we can, Mrs McAuliffe.'

'Mariella,' she told him, standing and shaking his hand. With the full light of the large window illuminating her, he could see that she was clearly much younger than her husband. She had a fine figure, long legs, a nose that reminded him of Sophia Loren, and an engaging smile.

'You are going to Gozo now? I will give you the number of my maid there, so you can call her and she can let you in.' She wrote the number on a pad, tore off the perforated page and handed it to Shilling.

'Do you have somewhere to stay? We have a guest suite at the Xaghra house that you could use...'

'We've booked him in to the Grand,' Galea told her.

'Then maybe I will see you there. I will need to go back to Gozo to collect some of my things.'

Heading for the door, Shilling paused and asked: 'That portrait... Are you really throwing it out? If you don't want it, could I please have it?' He thought a portrait of a Knight of Malta would make an excellent souvenir of his trip. Better, anyway, than a piece of tatty lace.

'I can't think why anybody would want a picture of that treacherous dog,' she said. 'But then, you are not Maltese. If you want it, please take it away, with my compliments. You'd be doing me a favour. I don't want it in the house.'

In the car Shilling reached round to the back seat where they had placed the files and the picture frame. He gingerly lifted the picture forward and rested it on his knees to study it. 'Hompesch...?'

'Last Grand Master of the Knights,' Galea told him. 'He was the one who surrendered to the French, without so much as a struggle. There were some excellent Grand Masters, and some courageous ones. But he wasn't one of them.'

'She's a good looking woman, our Mariella. She must be – what? – thirty years younger than her old man.'

'About that. She was Miss Malta, in her day. McAuliffe was a judge, or a sponsor, maybe both, in the contest. That's how they met. He left his first wife for her. Divorced in England, married in Malta.'

'And, more recently, he has a mistress?' It was a shot in the dark, but Ashe had said that adultery was a national sport.

Galea was equally in the dark. 'Oh... there will be one, somewhere, I have no doubt. We haven't found her yet, but something drove Mariella to drink...'

'To drink?'

'Didn't you notice how she kept looking at her wristwatch? She has a very strict rule: no alcohol before ten in the morning.'

'Ten o'clock? Jesus!'

At the ferry terminal he drove to the front of the queue, telling the attendant who was trying to keep the other traffic in order that he was 'police on duty'. He said the same thing to the marshal directing vehicles onto the boat and was directed to the front of the ship. They went up to the lounge bar and Galea asked: 'Beer?'

Shilling nodded and while he commandeered a table with a couple of chairs the Gozitan joined him with two yellow cans of lager and two plastic glasses.

'I was thinking... how much money...?'

'Quite... well, stacks of fifties and hundreds... twenty notes would be a thousand or two thousand. Two hundred, less than an inch thick, would be ten thousand or twenty thousand. So, about a million euros, at a guess. Did a lot of cash transactions, did he, our John?'

'That was his reputation, yes. He wasn't the sort of man who usually left any paper trail of receipts.'

Johnny Cash, Ashe had said.

'And your bosses at Floriana all thought he was a bit of a lad.'

'Well, with loads of cash you can do anything or buy anything – including people – or even be anything. People will turn a blind eye to everything where cash is involved. Cash is untraceable.'

'Yes, well everybody on Malta was turning a

blind eye and this bugger was arming terrorists all over Europe.'

'Money talks, bullshit walks,' said Galea.

'Bullshit certainly walks through Malta.'

Their car was first off the ferry when it docked in Gozo and they drove in a roundabout route through small villages to the general hospital, Galea explaining that the main road from the harbour to the city was being rebuilt from end to end.

'And they prefer to leave that sort of work for the tourist season, do they?'

'You must understand, it rains a lot in winter, which is why our island is so green.'

'And now the sun is shining, but nobody is working on the road.'

'Well, no... it's too hot for that.'

In the mortuary a doctor slid out a drawer containing McAuliffe's naked body which he transferred to an examination table.

The skull had been opened and reclosed. He pointed to a small mark.

'Here is a contusion from a smallish, curved but heavy object. A bang on the back of the head, sufficiently hard for it to have bruised the brain. It could have caused a loss of consciousness, at least temporarily...'

'But not hard enough to have caused the fatality?'

'We don't think so. And here, the little finger of the right hand, bent back with sufficient force for it to break at the joint. My opinion was that this is what probably did the fatal damage, the shock from the pain of that assault bringing on a heart attack. He probably wouldn't have known, but he was a prime contender for it. Weak heart... And here... pressure marks on his lower arms that we referred to the forensic pathologist who concluded that they were consistent with being tied or more likely strapped down.'

Shilling asked for the loan of a magnifying glass and examined the indentations. 'Something flat with sharp edges,' he said. 'Like a belt. Was McAuliffe wearing a belt when you saw the body?'

'Not wearing it,' said Galea. 'It was coiled in his lap.'

'So... strapped down with his own belt. That's one arm. And the other arm...' he peered again through the glass. 'Same thing. Maybe the assailant's belt. But of course he would have taken that away with him when he left the scene, otherwise his trousers might have fallen down while he was making his escape. Any fingerprints on McAuliffe's own belt?'

'I am not sure that we would have looked for them, there.'

'Might be worth... oh, bugger... we've given it back to the wife, haven't we? So there'll be no point in dusting it now.'

The officers thanked the doctor and as they drove out of the hospital complex Shilling said he was surprised that an island the size of Gozo could maintain a general hospital.

'Yes, we're lucky, in a way, with only twenty-four thousand regular residents. But sadly it's a bit of a dump. Thirty cleaners but I don't think they have a mop or a duster between them.'

A barrier pole was lifted for them at the entrance.

'See that? How many people do you think they employ to lift that pole? I'll tell you: a hundred and ten. And how many police officers do we have on Gozo? One hundred and ten.'

'Look on the bright side,' Shilling told him. 'You've never had an ambulance pinched.'

They travelled back towards the harbour by a different but equally circuitous route.

Under the portico of his hotel Shilling collected his picture and the files from the back seat. Galea said he would be back in the evening, and take him somewhere decent for dinner.

'By the way,' he said, 'At some time you'll need to talk to the investigating magistrate.' Noting the expression on Shilling's face, he continued, 'That's the way we do things here. In theory he's in charge. But don't worry. He'll come to see you. That way you can buy him a drink.'

Shilling checked in, collected a key and took the lift to his room. He threw his bag and his jacket on the bed, put on his new straw hat and went out onto the balcony to sit in the sunshine, admire the view across the channel to the Blue Lagoon of Comino, the mile-square island between Malta and Gozo, and start reading the papers he'd taken from McAuliffe's safe.

Four

To have described John McAuliffe, as Ashe had done, as a 'Mr Fixit', Shilling now realised, was a massive understatement. The man was a mover and shaker on a world scale, corresponding with people at top level in governments in Angola, Namibia, Tanzania, Congo, Nigeria, Ethiopia, Chad, Libya, Tunisia, Mali, Algeria... as well as in Palestine and Somalia.

And his end-users included names and addresses in England, Ireland, France, Germany and Italy.

A stack of receipts and invoices clearly showed that McAuliffe provided arms and ammunition to some, and what were described as 'security services' to others. His problem appeared to be, however, where he had not provided services, but had charged for them. There was correspondence, including handwritten notes of telephone calls, about these discrepancies. Perhaps this could be the explanation for a visit to his home by a stranger, resulting in his death.

Many of the English and Irish names were vaguely familiar to Shilling. They would be well-known to his chums in the sneaky-beaky brigades, in Anti-terrorism, Special Branch and MI5. But knowing the names was never enough; what those guys needed was firm evidence, and in this sheaf of papers Shilling probably had sufficient to put a fair number of them behind bars.

He felt slightly puzzled by the widow's readiness to part with so many of the documents her husband had felt necessary to keep in a safe. Was she naive, or simply disinterested in her husband's business dealings? Was she aware of what was going on and eager to make a clean break, a fresh start, to wash her hands of illegal business transactions and carry on without it? After all, she had something like a million euros stashed in the safe at home, and there would presumably be more in the bank. She wasn't going to be short of a few quid for a long time coming.

As he read each document Shilling stacked three different piles. There was the gun-running and explosives stack, another on non-arms-related transactions with mainly African states, and a third pile that dealt solely with the movement of large amounts of money.

He moved from the baking heat of his balcony back into the shade and the air-conditioning of his bedroom and called the reception desk to ask whether they had a photo-copier he could use. The girl said that if he left the documents with her she would get them copied for him. He thanked her and said he would think about it.

He found Ashe's card and called him next. A professor of history would surely have a photocopier.

Unnecessarily, he reminded Ashe who he was and when they'd met. It had been only the previous afternoon. Then he said that he was on Gozo and in need of a copying machine. Did Ashe have one? Or maybe a scanner-printer connected to his computer? Ashe said that he did indeed have such a device, but added that it wasn't very reliable and he was actually thinking of investing in a new machine.

'A better idea, then...' suggested Shilling. 'Suppose I buy a printer-scanner – just a fairly basic but reliable model. Would you be interested in buying it from me, say for half what I pay for it, when I leave the island? Ashe said he certainly would, so Shilling decided that the computer shop would be his first port of call in the morning. The second would be to buy a pair of shorts.

He was sitting on the street-level terrace, halfway down a pint of local lager and watching the sun set behind an English-looking church spire, when Jesmond Galea arrived to pick him up for dinner. He pulled out a chair to join him and a waiter appeared beside the table. Shilling had clocked the name badge on his claret-coloured waistcoat, so he said: 'Ah... Paul...'

The waiter looked at him then nodded at both men. 'Mr Shilling... *Sur*-inspector... A refill?'

'Two of these,' said Galea. As the waiter retreated he asked whether Shilling had found anything interesting in the McAuliffe files, and Shilling told him about the three piles he had made.

'You are making copies for me,' said Galea. It wasn't a question.

'I have thought about that. Of course you can and must have copies of everything. It's your investigation, not mine. But I want you to sit on the arms dealing stuff for the time being. For one thing, your guys at Floriana made it very clear to me last night that they are not involved and not interested in that side of the business. More to the point, if I give you copies and they go into your system, God knows where they will finish up. And I don't want anybody to be tipped off about what we know – what I know – before I have got the information back to London and they've had time to read it and respond to it.'

Galea appeared to be slightly offended at what might be interpreted as a slur against members of his force, but Shilling thought he had got the point across.

'On the other hand, some of the dealings about where he was selling people short, especially Africans and Arabs, could have a bearing on the case we are investigating, so I will, of course, show you those and point them out and make extra copies of those documents.'

Galea thought for a moment about what he was hearing, then said:

'You know, it isn't necessarily out of order for somebody to charge for a job that they are not actually doing. Sometimes this can be a method of paying extra, on the side, for a job maybe in the form of commission. But it may need an invoice and a receipt. It may be that there was no job – which would explain why he didn't do it.'

'Is that the way you move cash around in the Mediterranean, then? – To charge for jobs that you are not going to do and that don't need doing?'

'Sometimes it is. If jobs and payments need to go through the books. Naturally, if they are not going through the books, it is just a method of transferring cash.'

'Which may explain a million euros in a wall safe...'

'Precisely.'

Then, said Shilling, there was the matter of the movement of money – vast amounts of it, between Malta and banks in the Bahamas, Panama, Switzerland, the British Virgin Islands, and even the Vatican.

There were names – presumably of the account holders – attached to each transaction.

'Most of them have *Hon* in front of the name, so I guess they would be...'

'Politicians or members of the judiciary. No surprises there, although the evidence will be useful. They may be called Honourable, but most of them are in it for what they can make on the side.'

'Even judges?'

'Sometimes, especially judges.'

'So there's a possible motive of blackmail, I guess.'

'It's possible, yes. But why would he blackmail his clients? He would be charging commission anyway, wouldn't he? He doesn't appear to have been short of money.'

'Maybe it was the fear of potential blackmail. All these transactions, with real names alongside them in plain sight... maybe somebody wanted to remove the possible threat.'

Shilling said he would need to hire a car in the

morning. Galea asked why, when he was more than ready to drive him anywhere he needed to go on the case.

'I want to do some shopping while I am here. And maybe I'll do some sight-seeing at the weekend. I don't want to lumber you with that sort of chore. You're not my driver.'

They downed their pints and got into Galea's car for the short drive to the restaurant on the marina.

'I was surprised at Mariella's willingness to hand over the documents when we asked for them,' Shilling said.

'Why should she worry? My guess is she knows there's probably something illegal and wants it to be clear that she's not involved. A fine looking woman, though, eh? I wonder who'll be next into her bed. I'll bet there'll be a queue for that privilege.'

'You married, Jesmond?'

'I'm not... but my wife is...' He looked at Shilling to see whether he was amused by his response. If he was, it didn't show.

'... Yes' he said. Two boys... the wife is at home all day housekeeping and looking after the kids and moaning about the hours that I put in.'

'But I heard you don't work weekends, is that right?'

'Of course I do, when there's work to be done. And I'm on call twenty-four hours, too. And there's no overtime pay for officers.' He made a hairpin manoeuvre onto the marina road which was rutted with tractor tyre and caterpillar tracks. As they bounced along he said: 'Oh... the constables, you mean... well... they get overtime at weekends. There's a hell of a lot of road traffic to handle because the Maltese come over, and sometimes there's a fair bit of crime, that comes with them. But a young constable needs overtime to make up a living wage. The basic pay for a recruit hardly reaches the minimum level for paying tax.'

'So why not increase the basic pay, and put them on five shifts out of seven, so you can do away with the overtime, or most of it, and save money?'

'It wouldn't save money,' said Galea. 'Increased basic pay would mean higher pay for holidays, and sickness, and so on, and increased pensions. Plus, of course, a higher rate for overtime when it was needed. The budget wouldn't stretch to it. You need to understand that the pay rates here are nothing, compared with England. Our chief commissioner, chief of police, earns less than you do. Think about that.'

By chance, he said, there was currently plenty of opportunity for overtime shifts. There had been a spate of robberies on Sunday mornings. The police believed that teams of youngsters from Malta – local Gozitan youths wouldn't do that sort of thing and anyway they never got out of bed early at weekends – were watching in village squares as old people emerged from their homes for early Mass. As the worshippers entered the church the kids would go into their unlocked homes and steal anything they could find: usually cash or low-value jewellery. Its absence might not be noticed immediately and it was easy for a robber to hide on his person.

'Good Catholics, eh?' asked Shilling. 'Or would they be the odd four per cent that were not religious?'

'Not all Catholics are good Catholics,' said Galea. 'Or we'd all be out of a job.'

They parked and walked up to the restaurant, entering beneath the sign of a ship's wheel.

'You have a bit of skirt on the side, do you?' Ashe had said that most Maltese men did, and a police senior inspector working irregular hours would have plenty of opportunity to play away from home.

'Not especially. But who knows what the night might bring?'

It became patently evident what the night might bring when they entered the restaurant whose name, Galea said, could be translated as wheel, tiller, rudder, helm or helmsman. He shook hands with the restaurateur and introduced him to Shilling as 'Leli' which he said was short for Emanuel. Shilling realised that he would never fathom the language. As they were being shown to their table two young women arrived, kissed the owner, then walked over to be greeted by Galea, who also kissed them, and introduced them to Shilling.

The taller of the two, with shiny black trousers so close-fitting that they could have been sprayed on to her legs, said: 'Well, this is such a nice surprise, meeting you, out of the blue. We had just decided, on the spur of the moment, to make a girls' night out...'

To Shilling, it was obvious that there was no surprise whatsoever. The meeting had clearly been planned. And there was nothing 'spur of the moment' about the way the women were dressed and made up. The same thought had obviously occurred to Leli the restaurant owner, who asked whether they wanted to dine together, in which case he would bring up two more chairs. But he already had an extra chair in each hand when he asked the question.

In fact, they turned out to be amusing company. They asked him whether Scotland Yard bore any resemblance to the way it was usually portrayed on TV cop shows; when they heard that he intended to hire a car they suggested places that he should visit; and when Paulu, the owner's son, appeared bearing a tray of different varieties of fish they even recommended what Shilling should order. He had thought about going for duck, but Graziella, the girl who appeared less likely to be Galea's chosen date but was the taller and prettier of the two, told him he could eat duck any time in England; in Gozo he should eat local fish, and they agreed to share a small barracuda between them.

The unexpected – by Shilling – company meant that the two officers couldn't talk about the case they were investigating. But by the time they were half-way through their third bottle of Sicilian white he wasn't sure that there would have been much for them to discuss, anyway.

When the bill was presented the females clearly didn't expect to be paid for and Galea divided the total into four, each paying their own quarter.

Then Graziella suggested that she would give

Shilling a lift back to his hotel, while Galea could take her friend, who lived near him.

Shilling said he could easily walk the few hundred yards back up the hill, but Graziella insisted. And when they were back at the Grand she asked him to invite her in for a nightcap.

The hotel bar was closed, so she said: 'Well... they'll do room service. So let's go to your room and order from there.'

He had been fixed up, set up, by Galea. But why not? He had been living a virtual bachelor life for five years, since the day he arrived back home from an extended job in the north of England to find a note from his wife saying that she'd left him and gone to stay with a girlfriend from work, and a postscript reminding him not to forget to feed the cat.

He was a free agent, and what Galea got up to was not his concern. So he took Graziella's hand and led her to the lift.

She was gone when he was woken in the morning by the sun streaming in through the balcony window; the only evidence that she had been there being an imprint on the mattress and on the pillow.

He looked around him and saw the piles of paper. Shit! He had left them out so that anybody could have found and read them. He made a quick check. He was confident that they were all there. Why wouldn't they be? They were of no interest to Graziella who was, he now remembered, a hairdresser, and had promised to return, any time he called her, and trim his hair.

Nevertheless, it had been a pretty reckless idea to leave the documents on the table. He called reception and asked them to reserve him a safe deposit box.

Five
Il-Gimgha

As Galea's car forked off the main village-centre road and headed for the coast, followings signs that said *Knisja Nazzarenu,* which he said translated as Church of the Nazarene, Shilling laughed and said: 'Well... nobody could accuse your Roman occupiers of having built these roads...'

'What do you mean?'

'Look at them... narrow and dog-legged. What would be wrong with building a bit of straight road, now and again, with room for vehicles to pass?'

Galea was clearly becoming peeved by his English counterpart's constant criticism of his native island. And, in truth, Shilling was aware of it himself, and wondering whether he was piling it on too thickly; he thought that maybe Professor Ashe had had too profound an effect on his thinking, not least because he was already developing a fondness for the smaller Maltese island. What little he had seen of it, and of its inhabitants, he really liked.

'Let me explain,' said Galea, pointedly patient: 'First, the streets are narrow because narrowness provides shade. This isn't like England where, if you are lucky, the temperature in midsummer is lower than we are normally used to during our winter months. Here, the sun scorches, and burns, so the buildings block out the sun.'

He negotiated a sharp left and right jiggle in the

road, and then continued: 'And what you call the dog-legs were built for a purpose. If you are likely to be invaded, all those little corners, and the maze of narrow streets and alleys, serve to protect the residents, to baffle the invaders, and to deflect arrows and gunshot. You can retreat towards your home and the people chasing you can't get a clear shot. That's something else that you English cannot understand. This tiny island has been invaded many times, not only by the Turks but also by pirates, and they sometimes took as many as four hundred or five hundred people at a time into slavery on their galleys. And sometimes, if they were important people, they were held until somebody paid a ransom to free them.'

Another history lesson, thought Shilling. At this rate he would soon be an expert like Ashe.

The McAuliffe's Gozitan maid, swathed in mourning black, was waiting at the house for them and took the two policemen to the reception room where the body had been found. Galea opened the shutters to admit some daylight, then opened the folder of photographs he was carrying, put it on a table and rearranged some of the furniture to match the scene as it had been when the police cameraman had arrived.

He pulled a heavy leather-cushioned wooden chair into the centre of the room.

'There had been no signs of a break-in. So whoever came in was either invited in, or forced their way in when the door was opened for them. McAuliffe was sitting here,' he sat in the chair, '...like this, his head lolling to one side... like this. As you can see, he was wearing a short-sleeved shirt and his arms were dangling down the sides of the chair... like this. His belt was out of the loops of his trousers and curled up in his lap....'

Shilling looked at the photos and nodded. He had got the picture.

'Now this...' he picked up a bronze statue, about ten inches tall, of a Knight of Malta holding a shield in one hand and a sword in the other.... 'This is what we think did the damage to his head. There were no prints on it, and no skin or hair traces, but the pathologist thought the base could have been used as the weapon that caused the head wound. He said it wasn't conclusive, though.'

There was another big bookcase. Shilling tried to shove it, first in one direction, then in the other. It didn't budge. He opened the glass doors and looked at a couple of volumes.

'The glass doors are to protect against humidity,' said Galea. 'Sometimes it can be ninety per-cent here, or even higher.'

Shilling gingerly extracted one of the old volumes and read the title aloud: *'Il Gozo Antico-Moderno e Sacro-Profano Isola Mediterranea adiacente a Malta Africana...'*

'Gozo ancient and modern, sacred and profane,' Galea translated, 'by De Soldanis.'

'Yes; I'd worked that out.'

'That's the original Italian version, very valuable now. But you can buy an English translation in the bookshops.'

Shilling pulled out another. It was in Spanish. 'Balbi's *Siege of Malta,*' said Galea. 'Published in 1568. Written by an Italian soldier who took part in the battle.'

'Two presumably rare and valuable books,' said Shilling. 'But our burglar wasn't interested. Nor in anything else that we can see, here.'

'He was looking for a safe again, though. The pictures had been moved again, same as in the Birgu house.'

The telephone was on a table in the same room. Shilling walked over and sat in the leather chair behind it.

'So at some time on his last day he would be sitting here using this table as his desk when the phone rang and he made a note: *TF* – telephone call from – *Vatman 8*. So who the hell is Vatman 8?'

He stepped out of the front of the house into a street; it was still narrow but slightly wider than the others in the village suburb.

'Did you do door-to-door?'

'What?'

'Did anybody speak to the neighbours, ask them whether they saw or heard anything unusual, maybe a car that wouldn't normally have been parked outside or nearby?'

'No. But people round here keep themselves to their selves.'

'We have nothing better to do. Let's do it now.'

'Today is Friday. You are talking about Monday night. How on earth would anybody remember?'

Shilling re-entered the house and emerged

holding a TV guide. He quickly flicked through the pages then scanned the columns for Monday. 'We're talking around eight to nine o'clock, right? Tell them what they were watching on TV and see whether that prompts their memory.'

Taking different sides of the street and knocking only on the doors of houses that might have been within earshot, the job was soon completed.

'The guy in that house,' said Shilling, pointing at a door, 'says his TV viewing was interrupted several times by a dog barking on a rooftop. So maybe we might assume either that there was a stranger in the street, or perhaps that there was somebody in one of the houses shouting and upsetting the dog.'

'Yes... I suppose an Englishman might assume something along those lines,' Galea said, shaking his head as if in despair. 'Except that there's a barking dog on a roof every night in every street in Gozo. You'll see, or hear, that for yourself if you stay here long enough. So I'm afraid it's no help whatsoever.'

The two men returned to the hotel and sat on the terrace drinking lager, their conversation interrupted every few minutes by lorries, clearly overladen with gigantic rocks being taken from a coastal quarry to the ferry and then to Malta, and by concrete mixers and earth movers pounding at speed down the hill before slamming on their brakes at a sharp right-angled bend on the junction with the main road to the harbour. They had an appointment with the examining magistrate, Scicluna, at three o'clock.

He arrived as the church clock opposite struck four.

'I appreciate that, under your system, you are nominally in charge of this investigation, but...'

'Not nominally. Absolutely. I take charge of material witnesses and of material evidence.'

'...But we don't have much to report. There are no material witnesses that we know of, other than the perpetrator or perpetrators who we haven't identified and the victim who is of course unable to testify. And the material evidence, such as it is – and that's possibly a statue of a Knight that he might have been hit with, a trouser belt that he was strapped down with, and a diary in which he made what so far as we know was his last note ever – you haven't hung on to. Not, I gather, that it would make much difference if you had.'

'And meanwhile Chief-inspector Shilling has recorded the instance of a dog barking on a roof, which he thinks may be significant...' offered Galea.

'A barking dog on a roof? A dog *not* barking on a roof... now that might be significant, if it ever happened...'

The two Gozitans smiled at each other.

'Okay. I get the idea. But it was around the right time. We think he died around nine o'clock, right? So say the assailant arrived a short time before that. Some time between eight and nine, anyway. But enough time to interrogate McAuliffe about what he wanted to know, and then to bash his head, and strap him up, possibly while he was unconscious, and break his finger when he recovered...' Shilling was moving his hands as if weighing the amount of time each piece of the action might have taken.

'I've got it! Some time during the day he gets a phone call from a guy and he makes a note in his diary: *TF Vatman*. And the guy asks to meet him at home at eight o'clock. So as a memo he writes an eight after the entry. That would explain the wording *TF Vatman 8*.'

'We still don't know who this friggin' Vatman is, though,' said Galea. 'We know he's not the accountant.'

'What sort of whisky did he drink?' Scicluna asked. 'Maybe it's the man who delivers him Vat 69. Anyway, it wouldn't be anybody from the VAT office, because in summer they all finish work at eleven-thirty in the morning.'

'How on earth does anything ever get done on this island? Or is it the case that nothing ever gets done?'

'Our English friend here flew out on the same plane as Duncan Ashe; he thinks we're all Arabs,' Galea explained.

'Ah, Profs... What would we do without him? I am serious, you know. Without Professor Ashe we might all think that we lived on beautiful islands with perfect amenities, in our island paradise. We need Profs and people like him to tell us where we are constantly going wrong.'

The magistrate helped himself to one of Shilling's cigarettes.

'And when I visit England I think what a pity it is that there is nobody like Professor Ashe there, to point out how the place is falling apart, and maybe point out the Arabs to them, too.'

'Your local chronicler, De Soldanis, clearly thought that Malta was African, and Gozo was only adjacent to it,' Shilling told him, ignoring magistrate Scicluna's obvious sarcasm.

The magistrate raised an eyebrow in surprise that Shilling had heard of De Soldanis.

'Well, we are obviously the border between Europe and Africa. Maybe we are Arab,' the magistrate told him. 'In which case we should be proud of our inheritance. The English, with no culture of their own, look towards the Romans and the Greeks, but it was the Arabs who gave us geometry and astronomy and science and numbers. The Romans had no concept of zero – that came from the Arabs, you know.'

'That's ridiculous,' said Shilling. He thought for a moment, then asked: 'If a Roman has three apples, and you take two of them, then you take the remaining apple, how many apples does he have?'

'He has no apples,' replied the magistrate.

'He has zero.'

'No; he has no apples. He doesn't have any apples to count. The Arabs understood mathematical zero and if we are descended from them, it puts us ahead of the game.'

'What you are saying is that you Maltese understand the meaning of absolutely nothing.'

'Exactly,' said the magistrate.

Scicluna left them, feeling that he had won an argument and taught an Englishman something, parting with a request – an instruction – that he be kept up-to-date with the investigation. Paul the waiter appeared with two more pints and a set of car keys that he handed to Shilling.

'They brought your hire car while you were talking. It's in the car park.' The writing on the key fob said it was a blue Hyundai with a K registration.

'Didn't he want to see my licence? What about signing for it, and the insurance?'

'Oh, you can do all that paperwork when you hand it in,' Galea told him.

'And if you haven't had an accident you won't need to fill in the insurance forms or pay for cover. So you will save a bit of money.'

'This island... incredible... I love it!' said Shilling, and he nearly choked as he laughed and took a swig of lager at the same time.

Galea had given him directions to the shops he wanted to visit, so he drove into town – the diversion signs led him in a different direction from his previous route, and often seemed to expire altogether so he twice found himself in a cul-de-sac. Eventually he simply followed the traffic and made his way to a picture framer's shop.

He produced his print of the Grand Master with the cracked glass and the man, seemingly unimpressed by the portrait, said he could fit a new piece while Shilling waited. He took a scalpel from a drawer and scored the brown tape that held a backing card to the frame. This he removed, then a piece of battered material that the shopkeeper told him was possibly papyrus probably just there as padding to make a tighter fit inside the frame; he said people sometimes put a vegetable matting behind valuable pictures to absorb humidity and to protect against damage by insects such as silverfish, although they didn't normally bother with pictures like this, which appeared to be merely a photocopy of an etching. He replaced it with a piece of vellum, cut a sheet of glass to fit the frame and polished it, then retaped the back and put it, and the old padding, into a large envelope which he handed to Shilling in exchange for three euros.

He dropped the package on the back seat of his car and walked a few yards further to the computer shop, where he bought a small neat printer and photocopier, two packs of copying paper and some cardboard folders. He put the purchases in the boot of the car and then walked to a bookshop.

When he returned to the car he found a parking ticket on the windscreen.

There was a message waiting for him at the hotel when he returned to reception. Mariella McAuliffe had phoned and asked him to call her back.

He called her from his room, holding the phone in one hand while using his other to drop his trousers to expose his legs to the sun. It was still hot outside and he wanted to catch the last rays on his balcony.

She said she was back on Gozo and it had occurred to her that, if he was alone and at a loose end that evening, he could join her for dinner and maybe something else might come up that might help him with the case.

It would be a simple supper and a few glasses of wine, she said.

'Just the two of us. Nothing special, just pot luck.'

Shilling said he would be more than happy to join her, and hoped that he would be able to find his way back through the narrow winding streets. She said eight o'clock and Shilling thought about it for a moment, and then wrote in his notebook: *TF: Mariella 8*.

He took his Maltese souvenir picture out of its envelope and on to the balcony to admire in the sunshine. The portrait itself was inside an oval and he noticed what he hadn't spotted before – that within a ribbon painted at the apex of the hand-drawn inner frame were the printed words *Fr Ferdinando Hompesch* and *LXIX Gran Maestro.* At the base of the frame was his coat of arms, four crosses – upright in the top left and bottom right quadrants, X-shaped at top right and bottom left.

He checked the size of the frame against his wheelie-bag; it would just fit inside comfortably. He would keep the bit of old papyrus in an envelope and study it later; he had never seen papyrus before.

He set up his new copier-printer, but realising that every sheet would need to be copied individually, decided to leave the job until morning.

Just before eight he found the Xaghra house and the widow McAuliffe opened the door to admit him. She was, he noticed, dressed all in black. Black high heels, black stockings, short black skirt and loose fitting black halter-neck top. She even had a black ribbon in her hair.

'Pot luck' turned out to be fresh wild asparagus and a bottle of Sicilian chardonnay, followed by beef olives – thin slices of meat rolled and stuffed with onion, bacon, mushrooms, thyme and garlic, cooked in a sauce of mustard, carrot, celery and red wine, and served with vintage Tuscan red wine.

After dinner they moved to the room where she had found her husband's body. She didn't appear to be in any way affected by that fact. They sat side by side on a leather sofa and Shilling asked: 'If it's not too painful for you, could you just...'

She had, after all, offered more assistance with the case.

Of course, she told him. She had come home from playing bridge with friends in Victoria. The first thing that struck her was that he was sitting in a chair in the middle of the room. It was a chair he had never sat in previously, mainly because its proper place was at the opposite side of the writing table to his own chair. It was never in the middle of the room. He hadn't moved or spoken when she entered the room and her first thought was that he might be asleep and when she spoke to him her second thought was that he may have had a stroke. She moved towards him and immediately realised that he was dead.

'I mean... I didn't need to take his pulse or anything. It was absolutely obvious that he was dead. I went to take his hand and realised that his little finger was bent back at an impossible angle, obviously broken. I was going to call our doctor, I suppose to confirm formally that he was dead, and then I suppose to phone the undertaker. I wasn't sure what I was supposed to do. Then – I think I am recalling this in the correct order – I noticed a mark on the back of his head, and a spot of blood, and then his belt, not round the waist of his trousers but there on his lap. I think that may have been when I also noticed the paintings were off the walls. I don't think I had spotted that when I had walked into the room – I had been looking directly at John, I suppose. And that was when I thought I should call the police.'

'There are rare books on the shelves, and some of the paintings, I would guess, must be worth quite a lot of money. But you still say there's nothing missing?'

'Nothing that I'm aware of. Nothing at all.'

'One other thing. I am assuming that all these oil paintings are valuable. Why would he have had a print – and of Hompesch, of all people – in the safe, while these others were hanging where anybody could take them?'

'I honestly can't think of any reason – unless of course it was to keep the dratted picture out of my sight. Or it might have been a Lodge thing. His Lodge dates back to the time that the Knights were in Malta. But I don't think so, because all his Lodge paraphernalia is in the drawers of his desk. Except for the regalia, and that is in his wardrobe.'

She handed Shilling the bottle and he refilled their glasses.

'While you are musing on all that information, tell me about yourself. Are you married?'

Divorced, a few years, now.'

'Regular girlfriend, back home?'

'No; nobody special.'

She moved along the sofa, so close to him that their thighs touched, bronze flesh and sheer black nylon stocking-tops against cotton trousers.

'Let's open another bottle, shall we?'

'That would be very tempting, but I have to think about driving back. It wouldn't do, if I were stopped. I'm a police officer, remember.'

'There's no need for that. I told you yesterday that you could stay here, if you so wished.

Of course... she had mentioned that the house had a guest suite. But he knew that wasn't what she had in mind.

Rule One in the coppers' code of conduct was: Never have sex with a witness or a suspect.

However, mention of a bottle reminded him of something.

'In the scene-of-crime photographs there had been two crystal glasses on the writing desk, but no bottle. Somebody was obviously sitting over there drinking with your husband. Do you know what they were drinking?'

'It would have been whisky. John called it the Fiddich.'

He stood and walked over to the drinks tray: gin, vodka, an unopened bottle of Famous Grouse but no bottle of Glenfiddich.

'So... where's the bottle?'

'I don't remember seeing one,' she said.

'But if it was empty the maid might have taken it away.'

'Not before the photographs were taken.'

She said the maid may have taken it home later. Her husband kept bees and she would sometimes take him the empty whisky bottles to use for honey. It was recycling, and therefore good for the environment.

'Can you phone her and ask her whether she moved it, or took it home?'

She telephoned and the maid said she was certain that there had been no whisky bottle on the desk near the glasses. She hadn't removed any drink bottles since the break in and hadn't taken any home for more than a week.

So... the mystery of the missing bottle of Scotch...

Shilling looked again at the base of the bronze statue. It would be roughly the same diameter as a whisky bottle. If the statue could have been used to smash McAuliffe on the head, the weapon could just as easily have been the bottle from which the two men were drinking. But the thief, the murderer, had fairly obviously taken it away.

Why? For Dutch courage? Or because he realised it might be evidence?

They shared a parting kiss on the lips and he drove back to the hotel carefully, having no idea what the traffic cops on Gozo might be like although he was fairly certain that their attitude to drink-driving might be slightly more relaxed than that of his colleagues in the Met.

He thought about Mariella and wondered what – apart from the fairly clear offer of sex with a stranger while her husband's body was still warm – was going through her mind.

If she was saddened by his death she didn't show it. Perhaps she only realised the need to get on with her life as a rich widow.

While waiting for the lift after parking his car in the basement, he thought to himself: Love it or hate it, Malta is definitely the place to come if you're desperatc for sex.

Six
Is-Sibt

Shilling fell asleep on his bed while reading a paperback he had bought that afternoon, *The Great Siege*, written by Ernle Bradford, an Englishman.

He woke with a start around two o'clock. He had no idea what woke him (although Galea suggested later that it was probably a dog, barking on a roof). That piece of scrap that John McAuliffe had used to pad the portrait in a picture frame had weird symbols on one side. Mrs McAuliffe, when he'd asked her about the strange 'padding', said there might be some connection with the Knights.

The Knights were fighting the Turks in 1565 (and at most other times of their existence). Maybe the writing was Turkish; perhaps it would reveal something about the Siege. It could be some information about the battle that was hitherto unknown, or it might be a document that confirmed some assumed fact. Either way, it could be a piece of history.

He could make a gift of it to Ashe, as she had suggested after he mentioned his casual meeting with a historian, or if it turned out to be of interest maybe even to the national museum. She had given the picture, and the frame, and consequently whatever was inside the frame, to him, she said. It was of no interest to her.

He got out of bed and retrieved it from its

envelope. He had no idea what Turkish writing looked like. He didn't think it looked like Greek or Cyrillic. If he had to make a wild guess he would have made a stab at Persian. But if it turned out to be Turkish... anyway, he thought that Ashe would know.

He put the document into a drawer, went back to bed, read for a few more minutes and was soon fast asleep.

One good thing about the Mediterranean was that the shops opened early, so before breakfast he drove into town – the diversion route was different, again – and found a shop where he could buy a pair of shorts. The purchase had taken maybe ten minutes, but there was a parking ticket on the windscreen of his car when he came out of the shop, and no traffic warden in sight.

Back in his bedroom he pulled the table close to the sliding doors and set up the copier so that he could reach the pile of papers, load them one at a time onto the copier, make copies and create fresh stacks, all while sitting in the sunshine on his balcony.

By the time that Galea arrived to join him, and to order a pot of coffee from room service, the copying work was finished.

Shilling asked whether he knew what Turkish writing looked like and the Gozitan told him the Turks used the Roman alphabet nowadays, but that ancient Turkish was 'all squiggles, similar to Arabic scripts'.

'Look what I've found...' Shilling opened the

drawer and showed Galea the piece of paper padding.

'Papyrus,' said Galea, feeling the fabric between his forefinger and thumb. 'So whatever it is, it is very old.'

'McAuliffe was using it to pad out the print, in the picture frame she gave me. You're my witness on this one, cock. She gave me the frame after she cracked the glass, plus whatever was in the frame – right? I told her about it and she wasn't concerned. But I'm thinking that the paper... the papyrus... might be valuable. I mean, not so much financially as historically. In which case I could have it translated and maybe give it to the national library, or something.'

'It doesn't look much like what I remember as old Turkish,' Galea said. 'More like one of the Semitic languages. But in any case it would be worth only a few euros, so why should she be bothered? If it was just a plain piece of card or paper, she was obviously including it in what she gave you. I don't see that it makes much difference. Except that, maybe, if it is interesting in any way, maybe she might like to present it to the library or the museum herself. It's not like she needs the money. Anyway, how are you going to get it translated?'

'That Englishman, Ashe, that I met on the plane. He's a historian; I thought he might know.'

'Oh yes... Profs: well that's as good a place as any, to start. Meanwhile, can I remind you that we have a murder...?'

Shilling pointed to the stacks of paper. 'I haven't

been idle. These are original documents that deal with arms dealing within Europe, that I intend to take back with me.... I think they might be evidence of crime but as I told you it doesn't affect Malta.... these – and there's a set for you – are about disputed payments from his customers. I think it would be a good idea for you to show them to your special branch people in case the dispute could be a motive for a killing... and these are what look like tax avoidance or money laundering or both and will interest your fraud and revenue people. The rest are just company documents that I have copied, but that I'll give to the widow because, along with the disputed payments, I guess the company will need them and will have to decide what to do about them.'

Galea said he would go through the documents himself, first: 'At least that's something I can do at home. Keep the wife quiet by working at home. By the way, I had a thought last night. About *Vatman 8*. Maybe the eight wasn't an appointment. Maybe it was the time of the call.'

'As far as we know, he didn't usually note the call times.'

'No. But most of them would be during the working day. This one might have been remarkable because it came at night, after hours.'

'Could be, but it doesn't help much. I have had another thought, which if true is even less helpful to the inquiry. We have two break-ins, maybe concurrent – two separate teams of people – maybe consecutive, just one person or one team. First Malta, then Gozo, or maybe the other way round. And nothing stolen...'

'Let's assume Gozo would be second. You might lose the appetite for a second go at robbery if you have a dead body on your hands.'

Shilling agreed and sipped his coffee. Galea was sitting indoors, in the shade of the bedroom, while Shilling was still out in the sunshine.

'Nothing was stolen... as far as we know. But suppose the thief or thieves found what they were looking for... and it hasn't been missed, yet. Or the widow didn't know that it, whatever it was, existed in the first place...'

'You're right. That would be unhelpful. We are already getting nowhere, and that would put us further back than we started. My super wants a result. We have a rich man, a well-known businessman, found dead in suspicious circumstances and we have absolutely nothing to report. And nor has he. So he has his superiors, in Malta, on his back, and I have him on mine. He thinks that between us, Malta's finest and the famous Scotland Yard, it should be a doddle.'

'We can't rule out our blackmail theory but I think our best bet is that it's something to do with him fiddling one of his Arab customers who then come over either to deal with him and punish him for it, or to get their money back, or both. Can you check with special branch about which north Africans have been in and out of Malta this week? There'll have been lots of them, I expect, but I mean anybody who is known to them as being dodgy.'

'Not easy, but I'll get on to it on Monday. What are you doing for the rest of the weekend?'

'Today I am seeing Ashe at lunchtime, so I can ask him about that papyrus. Then I thought I might have a drive round the island and see the sights.'

'It's always very busy here at the weekend. Lots of Maltese come over.'

'I don't mind. I'm not in a rush. I'll just tootle about... the way most of the people here seem to be doing. Which reminds me...' He stepped indoors and crossed the room to his dressing table drawer. Can you do something about these bloody parking tickets? I seem to get one every time I stop the damn car?'

'Ah... K-reg... Hire car. Yes, easy meat for the wardens because they go on the hirer's credit card after he's left the island. So there's no come-back. No dispute. Give them to me, I'll sort them out. Which reminds me... hire car... I checked the number of that Escort in Birgu that we saw. It was rented by the Curia, so I suppose all it was would be a priest, probably calling on the widow before we arrived. Nothing sinister in that, I'm afraid.'

'You should take care,' Ashe told him as he poured a glass of wine. 'The tops of your legs are burnt. Look how red they are.'

'I know. But I was only in the sun for less than an hour.'

'It's African sun, this. It can burn the skin off a white man in a matter of minutes.' He waved his hand to summon a young woman who was walking among the other guests – some of them locals, others ex-pats – offering wine and who he introduced as his daughter, Vanessa.

'This is my friend Bob Shilling – yes, really, Bob Shilling – and, as you can see, he's only recently off the plane, hence the state of his legs. Can you find him some after-sun lotion, before his skin peels off completely?'

He relieved her of the wine bottle and took Shilling by the elbow and walked him under the shade of a gazebo on the cliff edge. 'We tend to stay out of the direct sun,' he said. 'It's okay for the natives, but a northern European can get enough sunshine from the reflected rays from the sandstone walls and the paving stones to give him a perfectly healthy glow.'

Shilling looked down and across to the island's port and marina, then over the sapphire-blue sea to the uninhabited island of Comino and beyond that to the northern shores of Malta.

'Wow!' he said. 'That is what you call a view!' He had spent all his life in cities; he had never given any thought to what people called scenery or landscapes, so he had never seen anything like it.

'Best vista in the Mediterranean,' said Ashe, proudly. 'You are looking at the point where Europe meets Africa. It is said by some – it's a nice idea but of course there's no evidence to support it – that before Noah's flood, when the Atlantic broke through into a valley close to what's now called Gibraltar, these two or three islands were mountains and were what people talk of as Atlantis. This place is full of self-aggrandising legends like that. Apparently after the Ark landed on Mount Ararat Noah's sons walked to Gozo. A good trek, that would have been. And there are what appear to be dual cart, or sledge, tracks in the rocks suggesting to some that at one time there was a land route from Sicily via Gozo and Malta all the way to Libya.'

'I have heard, or read, about that. Is it not true, then?'

'It could be, if you are prepared to believe that every journey followed precisely the same course within an inch either side sufficiently often to create and maintain the ruts in the rock. Otherwise, I have no idea what the marks might be.'

Shilling dug into the wide pocket of his new shorts and produced a piece of paper which he unfolded for Ashe, saying: 'I found this, yesterday. I thought it might interest you; thought it might be Turkish, maybe something to do with the Great Siege...'

The original document was too big to fit into any of his pockets, and not wanting to risk folding papyrus, he had taken the logical option of copying it on his new machine. In any case, he was more interested in its language and translation, than in the original.

'Not Turkish,' Ashe told him. 'Hebrew, or early Hebrew. I don't know, but I know somebody who will...'

He turned to Vanessa who was topping up their glasses. 'Could you find Mrs Field, sweetheart? And ask her to join us for a moment in my study?'

Mrs Field – Sarah – was short with dark hair cropped like a helmet and skin so bronzed and olive-toned that Shilling assumed her to be a native Gozitan. She flattened out the paper and studied it.

'Fascinating,' she said. 'Not Hebrew, but a form of Aramaic. It's the early equivalent of a wanted poster... what the French call a *signalement* and the English, in Sherlock Holmes' days, would have described as a *Hue and Cry*... But what's remarkable about this, is... Do you know what it is...?'

The Englishmen shook their heads.

'It's actually... Well... What you have here is a copy of the original warrant for the arrest of Barabbas, the rabble-rouser or insurrectionist who was arrested at the same time as Jesus.... I didn't know that this existed... In fact I have never been totally satisfied that Barabbas existed. I've never heard of there being a warrant issued for his arrest. Where is the original, do you know?'

Ashe said quickly that the whereabouts of the original could be discussed later. They just wanted to know what it said.

'It's a bit disjointed and distressed... some words missing... but... well... it looks like Barabbas also came from Nazareth. It says he is... was quite short... only three *ells*...'

'And an *ell* would be...?'

'Same as a cubit.... I suppose you want it in inches... Eighteen inches or a fraction more, based on the length of the arm of an average man, from finger-tip to elbow. So in English the man would be...'

'Less than five feet,' said Shilling.

'We do know that people of Nazareth were traditionally less than average height. But that may also be because he is, it says, *in appearance elderly* – obviously, from this, his age is unknown – and he has a stoop. But his beard is undeveloped, or immature, and his eyebrows meet above the nose... he has *a face from which spectators might shrink*... how's that for a description? And a long nose... scanty hair, parted in the middle... It is put out on the authority of Pilate. He was clearly not a fan.'

'But it sounds like he'd be easy enough to spot,' commented Shilling. 'Doesn't it mention the colour of his hair or eyes?'

'It wouldn't. Everybody's hair was more or less the same colour. Same with the eyes. The middle parting is, in itself, quite unusual – although it may be a guess, it actually says *in the manner of the Nazarenes* – because most men wore a turban or some other type of head-covering.'

Shilling asked: 'Does it say what the crime was?'

'I don't think it translates into English. It's a word just meaning a criminal. He was involved in some form of riot or civil disturbance. In Greek it would be *lestes...*' She looked enquiringly at Ashe.

'Bandit, leader of a mob, rabble-rouser... it's the word Josephus always used when referring to rebels or revolutionaries.'

She handed back the paper to Ashe. 'It would be wonderful to see the original. Is it in a museum, somewhere?'

'We're trying to find out,' Ashe told her. 'But first, we wanted to know what it said.'

'Well, when you find it, please let me know. I'd be fascinated to learn more.'

'That's enough New Testament history for today,' said Ashe, refolding the paper and passing it back to Shilling. 'Let's find my daughter and the drink.'

Quietly he said: 'Enjoy your drink today. I'll come to see you tomorrow and you are in for another history lesson, I fear. I've got a bit of research I'll need to do tonight. Please tell me that you've got the original papyrus somewhere safe...'

Shilling lied and said that he had. And hoped to God that hotel cleaners didn't check the drawers in bedrooms.

Seven

Shilling sat in his bedroom holding the piece of papyrus in awe. It was better than he had imagined it could possibly be. More historic than he had hoped for... and far more valuable than his wildest dreams. The warrant for the arrest of Barabbas... an artefact dating back to the time of Christ and Pontius Pilate...

But what would he do with it? What should he do with it? Its proper home, he felt sure, would be a museum. It would be great to have it on the wall of his bachelor apartment, no doubt about that, but it was possibly priceless. He could make a good photocopy of it, even copy it on to papyrus that he knew was sold in the better class of art shop, and hang the copy on the wall because, in the same way that some people had copies made of priceless jewellery and kept the originals in a bank vault, he felt that his new find was also priced beyond rubies.

He had heard about museums bidding millions of dollars for old masters and classic works of art. If he offered the warrant for auction, then the museum with the greatest interest could buy it from him, and everybody would be happy.

He studied the script carefully, but couldn't work out where the words were for Barabbas's height, or beard, nor even where the document said it had been issued by Pontius Pilate. But... no matter. He made another photocopy then placed the papyrus in one of his card folders, wrapped it in part of the polythene wrapping in which his copier had been packed, and took the lift to reception where he rented a safe deposit box and carefully placed it inside.

Then he strolled down the hill to Gleneagles, a waterfront bar that Ashe had said was the only decent pub on the island.

It was still early evening, but the bar was occupied in one corner by men he assumed to be local fishermen; a few obvious foreigners – French, Italian and Dutch – who were clearly yachties from boats in the marina occupied other tables, and a bunch of people who he thought looked local, but whose casual outfits all looked as if they were being worn for the first time, stood at the bar and he rightly guessed that they would be weekending Maltese.

The lone barman was busy but maintained a constant and infectious smile. When he eventually caught the man's eye he returned the smile and said 'Hi,' and asked for a pint of Cisk, the local lager, which he had learnt was pronounced Chisk.

'Hi,' returned the barman, who held out his hand and said: 'Welcome back.'

'My first time here,' said Shilling, shaking the man's hand.

'The barman appeared slightly confused, as if his memory was playing tricks on him. 'Welcome, anyway,' he said, grinning broadly.

Shilling took his pint and found an empty table on the balcony, which Ashe had also told him he should do, in order to admire the view and what he said was a unique quality of light on the fishing boats bobbing in the inner harbour. If Ireland had forty shades of green, he thought, this harbour must have forty shades of blue. The *luzzi* – local fishing boats with the eye of Osiris on the prow – were mostly painted in what was known as Madonna blue. Their reflection on the water changed the colour, and the varying depth changed it again. Reflection from the sandstone surroundings added a golden tinge and the wash from moving vessels lightened different patches of water by differing degrees.

Towards sunset, farmers who raced horses and sulkies along the island's main roads on feast days brought their animals down to the slipway, some of them in horseboxes and others led by a rein from the driver's window of a truck. As the horses simultaneously cooled down and exercised by walking against the water pressure, they changed the hues of the blues yet again. If an artist accurately captured the colours, Shilling thought, nobody would believe he had got them right.

He turned away from gazing at the marina and nodded at the middle-aged man with grey hair brushed back and a narrow grey goatee beard who was sitting, also alone, on the next table.

'Good evening.... fellow inmate from the Grand Hotel...'

They fell quickly into conversation, as lone travellers often do, and Shilling learnt that the stranger was actually a native of Malta, now living in Rome.

He said he was enjoying a working holiday,

researching a book he planned to write about freemasonry on his native island.

Shilling recalled that McAuliffe had notes in his diary about lodge meetings, so said that he had been surprised to learn that in a country that was reportedly ninety-six per cent Roman Catholic, there would be a freemasons' lodge.

'*A* lodge?' said the man. 'There are nine of them!'

'In a country of only – what? – four hundred thousand people, most of them Catholic? Nine lodges?'

'And that's only the official lodges. There are also a couple of unofficial ones. But you need to understand that most Maltese are Catholic in name only. Christenings, confirmations, weddings and funerals... it's only when they need it. I'm ashamed to admit that most of my countrymen are not what could be described as a God-fearing race.'

Shilling asked whether the man's researches had come up with the name McAuliffe.

He appeared to be thinking about it, perhaps mentally running through lists of names in his memory. 'In Maltese that would be Micallef,' he said. 'That's how you spell it and pronounce it.'

'No, this guy is English. The name is originally Scottish, possibly Irish. But it's McAuliffe.' He spelt the surname out.

'I can hardly be expected to remember the names of all the brethren, as they'd call themselves. But no... doesn't ring any bells.'

There had been a slight change in the man's demeanour at the mention of the name McAuliffe.

Shilling was a trained observer – he had been so described in court, dozens of times. What he chiefly observed were people, their attitudes and their responses when being interviewed: sometimes what they said was less important than the way they said it.

The Micallef-McAuliffe tangent was an irrelevance, playing for time. John McAuliffe was no Johnny-come-lately on the Maltese islands; he had been around and doing business for years; his name would have been familiar to most Maltese natives. Furthermore, the report of the death of so prominent a citizen had been on the front page of all the local newspapers that week; it seemed unlikely that he hadn't at least glanced at some of them. He could hardly have missed the story.

Shilling looked the man in the eyes. 'John McAuliffe? Prominent businessman? Died here on Gozo this week? It was in all the papers. You haven't heard about it, or read about it?'

He avoided the detective's stare and looked out to sea as if trying to jog his memory while studying the bobbing motion of the fishing boats below.

'When you put it like that... yes, I am sure I read something.'

'The police are treating his death as murder,' Shilling pressed on. 'Murder in the furtherance of theft. Used to be a hanging matter.'

'In the furtherance of theft? Was anything stolen?'

Scientists called it a Eureka Moment. Shilling called it a Got-Him Moment. This, he knew, was the man with the solution to his case.

'I don't know. The police aren't saying.'

Shilling offered his new companion another drink and stepped back inside the bar to order another pint and a glass of white wine. The barman said he would bring the drinks out to them and while they were waiting he introduced himself.

'By the way... Bob Shilling.'

'Loretto – Laurie – Pace.' Pronounced like patch.

He prompted Pace to tell him more about Malta's Masonic history, and learnt that it had been introduced to the island by the Knights of St John and these days included judges and magistrates, lawyers, politicians and senior policemen among its ranks.

Around sunset the two men walked together back up the hill to their hotel.

'So, what's your interest in Mr Micallef-McAuliffe?'

'Oh, I met his widow. She mentioned that he had been a member of a lodge and – before I met you – I had thought it strange, as I said, that there would be a lodge on a strictly Catholic island like Malta...'

But Pace knew there was far more than that behind Shilling's interest. He had seen him arrive at the McAuliffe house earlier in the week. Then, observing from a discreet distance, had watched him leave the house with a collection of paperwork and ledgers.

Back in his room Shilling thought: 'Got him...!'

But got whom or got what?

This man Pace was involved in the case, somehow. But involved in what way? Involved was a good word in policing. So was conspiracy. He was refreshing his memory about the rules of conspiracy which could be a last resort in crime-solving, or a useful catch-all, when the telephone interrupted his thought process.

It was Ashe suggesting a change of plan. Too many works of reference were involved in the story he wanted to tell him, so instead of Ashe coming to the hotel, Shilling should come to him.

That was no problem.

Shilling took the lift down to the basement car park. He checked the cars and made a note of the number of a hired silver Ford Escort. Then he called Galea at his home.

Eight
Il-Hadd

Ashe had cleared his desk and a long refectory table in his study and they were now covered in books, some open and others closed with their pages picked out by bookmarks in differing pastel shades.

His daughter Vanessa brought a tray containing a cafetière of brown-black coffee, a small milk jug, two cups and a plate of biscuits which she placed on a side table. 'Yell out when you want a refill,' she told them.

'Make yourself comfortable. Sit near the coffee. You won't need to take notes.' Ashe stood behind his desk, his fingertips resting on the black leather cover of the Bible, and began his lecture.

In 21st century Britain, he said, fundamentalism was a term most commonly applied to Moslems who quoted (and often misquoted) the Holy Quran in order to attempt to justify a violent act and it was therefore essentially a pejorative term. But for more than a hundred years Fundamentalism had been a Christian movement in the United States where it combined several theologies, rather than any single denomination.

Christian Fundamentalists believed in the inerrancy of the Bible, and in its infallibility. The Bible was The Word Of God, so it must be right, and its teachings must be followed.

'Fundamentalists may shuffle their feet a bit, hum

loudly and stick their fingers in their ears when confronted with the Old Testament laws found particularly in *Leviticus*: Don't cut your hair or shave; Don't wear clothes made of more than one fabric; People who have flat noses, or are blind or lame, cannot go to an altar of God; Don't have a variety of crops on the same field; If a man cheats on his wife, or vice versa, both the man and the woman must die. There are other similarly extreme laws in *Deuteronomy* and in *Timothy*,' he said.

'Well, those laws were basically rules of contemporary society, and times change. Nobody really, honestly, believes that God created the world in six days because, for a start, he was working before he had even invented the concept of a day. But the people who believe the Bible believe that he created it in six shifts. Fair enough. And yet... and yet... the real fundamentalists say that if the Bible says he made it in six days, it was six days, no argument. Because the Bible is The Word Of God.'

Then, said Ashe, consider the song from the musical *Porgy and Bess.* To look at only two verses, did Shilling – or anyone – believe that Jonah lived inside a whale, or that Methuselah, grandfather of Noah, lived 969 years? Ashe half-sang:

> *The things that you're li'ble to read in the Bible*
> *It ain't necessarily so...*

Nevertheless there were some who believed those stories for no other reason than 'Because the Bible tells me so'.

More common, however, was the number of

people who said they believed what was in the Bible, but didn't actually practice what it preached. For it appeared to be a truism that the more ostensibly holy or righteous or religious a nation may be (or profess to be), the more corrupt, violent and hypocritical would be its citizens.

Shilling knew what was coming next.

'Like over there in Malta?' – 'Precisely.'

Standing at a safe distance from the fundamentalists were the ordinary Christians and Jews – and others – who quite simply believed in God – that is, the God in the Bible. Whether lapsed, practising or devout, their worthy belief was that they should follow the basic laws of the Old and New Testaments. After Biblical readings in Roman Catholic churches came the phrase: 'This is the Word of the Lord'. And the congregation's response was 'Thanks be to God.'

'The problem arises here. For the Bible is not the word of the Lord, and certainly not The Word Of God, but the word of man,' Ashe said.

'Unlike the Holy Quran, which was dictated via the angel Gabriel from God to Muhammad over a twenty-three year period in the seventh century, the Bible is very much a man-made concept. And unlike archangels, men make mistakes. Even worse, when man thinks he has done something right, he has a natural tendency to go back to it and seek to improve it a bit.

'Take the Ten Commandments: a bit old fashioned perhaps, but most people would consider them to be a good set of basic rules for a civilised and religious community. Handed directly by God to Moses they have endured through the ages and were already ancient when Jesus himself decided they needed interpreting and updating.' Ashe put his finger on a bookmark and flipped open the Bible so that he could quote correctly.

> *You have heard that it was said to those of old, 'You shall not commit adultery'. But I say to you that whoever looks at a woman to lust for her has already committed adultery with her in his heart.*

That was in *Matthew*, chapter five, said Ashe.

There were similar alterations to the laws of murder and of swearing in oaths. If Jesus (the man) could not quote the Commandments – written in stone – without amending or improving them, what was the likelihood that a mere mortal, a scribe, faced with stories from an oral source, would be able to resist tampering with text?

But that was the way the New Testament had quoted Jesus, Ashe said.

'Actually, it is the way one – of the four – Gospels quotes Jesus. The other three (*Mark, Luke* and *John*) don't mention that the Son of God felt the need to update his father's words. Did they not think that it was worthy of note? Did they hear it but forget it? Or did Jesus not actually say the words that *Matthew* quotes?'

Nobody knew the answer. But what we did know was that although Matthew, Mark, Luke and John may have been disciples of Jesus (the Gospels say that they were), there was no verbatim shorthand and there were no recording devices, so the stories had to be committed to memory and repeated, and no doubt embellished along the way. And, doubtless, along the way parts of the story were omitted. Possibly they were deemed to be too complicated; possibly they were considered irrelevant to the plot; and possibly they were forgotten.

'And that reminds me,' said Ashe, 'about the wonderful story of the woman accused of adultery and about to be stoned. There was no mention of a man, but the penalty was the same for both participants. Unless you take Jesus's amendment literally, you can't commit adultery on your own. When he challenged her accusers, "Let he who is without sin cast the first stone," he was effectively letting the woman off. What was he saying? – That despite what was laid down in the Ten Commandments her adultery didn't really matter...?'

It would be seventy years after the birth of Christ that the first Gospel (the *Mark* version) was committed to writing (in grammatically poor Greek, said Ashe), probably a further ten years before *Matthew* appeared in Semitic-influenced Greek, maybe a further ten years before *Luke* was written (in elegant Greek), and it was possibly not until 100AD that *John* was committed to papyrus.

Apart from the fact that the New Testament said that John (like Peter) was illiterate, the great likelihood was that whoever wrote the Gospels, it was not the people whose names were ascribed to them.

The scribes who actually wrote them down

weren't present when the recorded events occurred; the Gospels are the stories as related orally by the Apostles, not written down by them..

Being human, some of the copyists made mistakes, and the people who copied those transcriptions also copied the errors. Worse, some of the scribes felt that part of the text may be unclear, so they amended it, no doubt sincerely believing that they were improving it. Worse still, there were scribes who thought that some of the content contradicted the plot, or the teaching of Christ, so simply removed it.

It was apparent that the writers of *Matthew, Luke* and *John* had access to *Mark*'s version when they were compiling their Gospels and they lifted some of his verses verbatim. *Mark* was almost certainly based on the preaching of Peter in Rome. Essentially, of course, they told the same story. But they differed slightly, because they were written for different audiences.

'It's only the New Testament that concerns us today. So let's start at the beginning,' said Ashe. 'I won't ask whether you believe in the concept of the Virgin Birth, which incidentally includes the belief, often overlooked, that Mary was herself also born immaculately, so that she had no original sin. That is purely a matter for your personal faith. But some biblical commentators have wondered why, if the story was known, Paul never mentioned it in his preaching. Others have commented that being fathered by the gods or by one god via a virgin was to some extent a basic requirement of great men –

Alexander the Great, Caesar Augustus... And you might think that the other writers, and not only *Matthew* and *Luke*, would have included it.'

The story was further complicated by the genealogies of Joseph, showing that he was directly descended from King David. The two Biblical versions were quite different, and some were in the wrong historical order – 'perhaps they had just been badly copied' – but if Joseph was not the natural father of Jesus, what did they matter?

'I fear that the answer is that the Virgin Birth did not appear in the earliest stories, but was a later addition. Look... I am not challenging anybody's faith, here, because it is of course possible that they learnt about it later from members of the family and thought it appropriate and even vital to include it.'

When did all this happen? *Matthew* says Jesus was born during the reign of Herod the Great, who died in March of 4BC.

Where did it happen? *Luke* says that everyone had to go to the city of their ancestors to register for a census, which meant Joseph travelling to Bethlehem. But the first census in Israel was in 6AD. Apart from the fact that there would have been no requirement for Joseph to take his heavily pregnant wife with him to register for it (because the head of the household's declaration would have been sufficient) it seemed a ridiculous idea to count people where their forefathers came from: a census was about where people lived and worked now, and where they paid their taxes. *Luke* said they travelled from their home in Nazareth; *Matthew* said they moved to Nazareth later. Both of them wanted the birth to be in Bethlehem, David's city, so they contrived an excuse to have them there.

'It seems fairly obvious that they didn't know where Jesus was born. But,' said Ashe, 'you'd think the writers of the Gospels would have got their act together, wouldn't you, so they would both, so to speak, be singing off the same hymn sheet?'

He paused to sip his coffee, then called for Vanessa and asked for a fresh hot brew. 'Does it all matter?'

He answered his own question: 'In many ways it does not matter one jot, because – and this is the important thing about the Bible, and especially about the New Testament – it is not, nor is it intended to be, a history book. It is a book not about history but about faith.... '

Where it mattered, he said, was when people said it was the truth – the Gospel Truth – 'because they can't both be right.'

He added: 'I suppose it is also worth mentioning, just in passing, that *Matthew* has the evil Herod slaughtering all the children in Bethlehem aged under two, in an attempt to kill the new-born Messiah. And yet the historian Josephus, who managed to chronicle so many of the evil doings of Herod, failed to mention the incident. But this would have been his greatest crime of all. So one is forced to wonder whether it actually happened.'

People believed it to be 'true history' because it was in one of the Gospels; they didn't doubt it because it wasn't in the other three.

'Where does this lead us? Only to the conclusion that the New Testament is unreliable as a source. The slaughter of the innocents would have been an amazing story as a sheer invention. If it is fiction, it was created only to emphasise the importance of the birth of Jesus. It is clearly not just a simple matter of somebody hearing a story but getting it slightly wrong.'

So much, said Ashe, for the beginning of The Greatest Story Ever Told.

'Now let's skip to the end. According to the first three Gospels, the Last Supper took place on the first day of Passover. *John* says that it was a day earlier, and that Jesus was crucified on the first day of Passover. See what I mean? They can't both be right, so which day was it?'

Does it matter? – 'Well, yes it does, because it is defining Easter for future generations, and around it the entire faith of Christianity revolves. And if they can't agree on which day it started…'

Ashe looked towards the door as Vanessa appeared there. 'I could go on…' he said.

'Oh yes, he could,' she said, smiling. 'And he will, given half a chance…'

Her father returned the smile and told Shilling: 'I could tell you that the Bible doesn't mention how many wise men there were, and that it never mentions a stable. But those were interpretations that were added by Christians down the ages, by laymen, not by the scribes.'

'He was born in a manger,' said Shilling.

'Yes. But this' – he crossed the floor to a trough-like niche in the wall of his study – 'this is a manger. Very common in Mediterranean lands. When these houses were built the animals were on the ground floor and the people on the first floor. That would be a good safe place to put a newly born baby, but it doesn't make this room or this house a stable.

'I could tell you that Jesus is quoted in the Bible as saying that Moses introduced circumcision to the Jews, although Moses didn't, it was Abraham, a mistake no Jewish boy, especially one who could debate the scriptures with the elders, would have made. Or that he said the mustard seed was the smallest seed on earth. But while there was a current saying about things being as small as a mustard seed, Jesus would have known that there were smaller seeds... Or that the New Testament had people make the equivalent journey of going from London to Birmingham by way of Penzance – because the guy who wrote the story had never set foot in the Holy Land!'

'Okay,' Vanessa told him. 'You have proved that you can go on. But lunch is ready. Just a snack. It's on the terrace.'

Ashe snapped his reference books shut and the two men followed her out to the gazebo.

Vanessa took a bottle of wine from a terracotta cooler and filled their glasses. 'I hate to change the subject when you are obviously so riveted by it. But have you had chance to see much of our island yet?'

Shilling told her the places he had driven to, and the sights that he had seen. 'Then you have seen more of it than some of the natives. Believe it or not there are people in this village, folk maybe as young as forty, who have never been to the other side of the island. Yet the longest journey you can make here in a car takes about fifteen minutes.'

Ashe nodded in agreement: 'I was talking to a local, a millionaire – there's no shortage of them here, incidentally, except you wouldn't know because they dress like peasants and never paint their doors, and they don't trust banks, so the most dangerous place for a Gozitan is in bed because there's usually so much money stuffed under the mattress that if they fall out of bed, it's from a great height…'

He took a breath. 'This chap, worth something like eighty million, told me he had been abroad once and he didn't like it. I asked him where he had been and he told me: "Malta". Just there, across that narrow stretch of water.'

They ate quails eggs and sardines, artichoke hearts, stuffed olives and anchovies, baby tomatoes, goats cheese and air-dried sausage.

Shilling lifted the wine bottle to look at the label.

'What do you think?'

Shilling, mouth full of delicious local bread, nodded his approval.

'Local chardonnay,' Ashe told him. 'An acquired taste, perhaps, but sadly I have acquired it. Does you no harm; won't get you pissed.'

'That's what he always says,' said his daughter. 'Which is his excuse for getting through five bottles a day. But sometimes I find him in the morning with his head in his hands complaining that there must have been something wrong with the sixth bottle, the previous night.'

As though concerned, she asked: 'How's the lecture going? Lost the will to live, yet?'

'Not at all. It's all fascinating. I suppose that, like most people, I have read the Bible only a bit at a time. It's probably only when you study all of it that you realise there are discrepancies in the stories.'

'Well, you are lucky... or not. Because he did Roman law as his first thesis. So he is on something of a hobby horse, I'm afraid. If he bores you, you can always come out and have a swim in the pool.'

'Yes; the Romans. We are just coming to them.' Ashe put his hand on Shilling's shoulder to lead him back to the study. 'Fill your plate and bring it with you.'

Nothing of what he had told him so far had been essentially bad, or evil. Human scribes made human mistakes. Everything was being written by hand, and the oral tradition had been remembered, not learnt by rote as a schoolboy might be expected to be able to recite tracts of Shakespeare.

Not even the introduction of printing could save it. In the early days every letter of the alphabet was in a different box – two boxes, because there were capital letters and lower case, and later there would be italic and bold type for each individual letter.

And when the job was finished the letters that had been used would have been replaced in their boxes. Working at great speed and often by candlelight, it was obviously easy to make mistakes: lower case *g* could be confused with *q*... capital *T* for

I or *J* or *Y; B, P* and *R* would all look alike, so would *G* and *C.*

And apart from that confusion there remained ordinary human error: mis-spellings and words accidentally missed out.

'Thus we got what was called the *Sinner's Bible,* where the word *not* was left out of the commandment about adultery. And in another version it says "Blessed are the placemakers", instead of peacemakers. My mother used to quote that one, every time she laid the table. It's amusing, I suppose, to recognise human frailty.

'The evil bit comes now,' he said. 'Or it starts now, with the reports of the trial or trials of Jesus.'

It was a well known story – how the disciples slept while Jesus prayed ('in a bloody sweat, according to *Luke,* although the others didn't include that interesting detail'), then Judas arrived with soldiers and temple guards and Peter drew a sword and sliced off the ear of a man who might have been called Malchus. And Jesus was taken to the home of the high priest – which was odd in itself, if Roman soldiers had arrested him.

It was important to remember that this episode followed Jesus' messianic entry into Jerusalem, where vast crowds had welcomed him and hailed the coming of the new kingdom, free of Romans, that he had promised.

This in itself would have greatly worried the priests who were far from popular among the masses, not least because they operated only under the sanction of the Romans, represented by Pilate.

Jesus was therefore, to put it mildly, likely to be a disruptive influence in the city during the most holy of Jewish festivals.

'In a city of normally twenty to thirty thousand inhabitants, there would likely have been more than a hundred and fifty thousand gathered for the feast. So the priests, not to put too fine a point upon it, would have wanted him out of the way. So – and this is only a theory to attempt to support any possibility of an official Jewish involvement on that night – suppose they intended to keep him in the priest's house, either under arrest or at least as an unwilling guest, for the duration of Passover. It may indeed even be the case that they intended to try him for blasphemy after the feast. What they couldn't possibly do – and this is where the early Christian chroniclers went wildly off the mark – was try him in advance of it.'

Anybody even vaguely familiar with Jewish customs would know that, at the start of Passover every single member of the Sanhedrin, from the high priest down, would have been – and was required to be – occupied, both in their homes and in the temple, with the cumbersome and complicated rituals for the preparation of the feast.

The idea that all seventy-one members could be summoned to, not to mention seated in, the high priest's residence in order to conduct a trial defied credulity.

In any case, based on what the Gospels told us, Jesus did not claim on his own account to be a divine being, or descended from God, nor did he claim on his mother's part immaculate conception or a virgin birth. Others may have made the claims on his behalf, and that might be why, if the priests had previously held any form of investigation (and a careful reading of *John* suggested that this might have taken place about a week before the feast), they encountered what were deemed to be 'false witnesses'.

As potential history, Ashe continued, the so-called Jewish trial was even more defective.

'The Sanhedrin could not exercise jurisdiction outside the temple court – certainly not in anybody's house. Criminal proceedings had to start and finish in daylight – not at night. They could not be held on the eve of, and certainly not on the day of, a religious feast. An accused person could not be convicted solely on his own confession, but required at least two truthful and independent witnesses.'

Interestingly, and although it must have been fresh in the priests' minds, with no shortage of witnesses, Jesus was not accused by them of violating the sanctity of the temple by attacking the money-changers.

'It follows, therefore, does it not, that the Jewish trial almost certainly did not take place, and would in any case have broken every rule in the book, if it did. While *Mark* (who seems to know little, and to care even less, about Jewish procedures) had a full-scale evening trial during a feast, *John* has no trial at all. Again... they can't both be right, can they?'

Meanwhile it also seemed highly unlikely that if Roman soldiers had made the arrest in the first place that they would have handed him over to the priests, pending trial.

Ashe refilled Shilling's wine glass, poured the remains of the bottle into his own glass and called to Vanessa that they would need another bottle in a few minutes.

'If you believe *John,* or give him the most credibility, it seems likeliest that the priests held an inquiry into Jesus' behaviour and – according to *Luke,* quoting Paul in *Acts* – found no behaviour to justify the death penalty – and, six or seven days later, Pilate sent a detachment of soldiers to arrest him for claiming to be king of the Jews, a title solely within Caesar's gift and currently bestowed upon the current Herod. But what is clear, at least from *John,* is that the Jewish trial and the Roman trial were not immediately consecutive.'

And that, he said, brought them finally to the arrest by soldiers on the warrant issued by Pilate: the little piece of papyrus that Shilling had innocently stumbled upon.

Nine

'It's a warrant for Barabbas,' said Shilling.

'Yes; I possibly appear to be getting a little ahead of myself, here. But think on this: without the involvement of Judas, Pilate and Barabbas, there would have been no first Easter. All three of them were required in order to fulfil the prophesy that the Messiah would be killed on the cross.'

When Jesus was brought before Pilate he was asked whether he was king of the Jews, and replied: 'Thou sayest it' – effectively, at least to Pilate, pleading guilty to the charge of revolting against Caesar by challenging the actual king appointed by and recognised by the emperor. As such, it amounted to an offence against *Lex Julia Majestatis*, treason against the Roman state or its people, enacted by the emperor Augustus in 8 BC, and was punishable by death. In Rome's colonies such a case would automatically be tried by a governor or procurator like Pilate who alone was invested with *jus gladii*, the right to pass and execute capital sentences.

If the accused was a Roman citizen, he could claim the right to be tried in Rome, or the procurator could transfer the case himself. That was of merely academic interest because Jesus was not a Roman citizen (although Paul, who appeared in the story later, was).

What the procurator could not do, said Ashe, was

refuse jurisdiction, and he certainly could not pardon an offender in the event of his being found guilty as charged. So if Pilate could not decline jurisdiction, nor delegate his powers to a lower or local or religious court because the *jus gladii* was invested personally in him, it threw the Biblical account somewhat into disarray.

'And what do we know about the character of Pilate?' Ashe thumbed a bookmark and opened his copy of Josephus' *Jewish War*.

Titus Flavius Josephus, he said, was born in Jerusalem in AD 37, so literally would have walked the streets that Jesus walked, and could easily have known people who knew or at least saw him. Having actually fought against Roman occupation, he eventually defected to them, becoming an official historian of Roman Judea. That did not, however, prevent his chronicling of Roman atrocities wherever he encountered them. And prominent among his list of villains was Pontius Pilate.

He recalled, for example, that while Pilate's predecessors had respected Jewish traditions, Pilate had gone to considerable lengths to offend them. He allowed his soldiers to bring their standards bearing effigies and images into the holy city and when a crowd gathered in protest had his troops surround them and threaten them with death. After holding out for five days it became obvious that the Jews would rather die than concede and submit to what they considered to be desecration of a sacred site, and he eventually backed down and had the images withdrawn.

Josephus also reported that Pilate spent the Temple's money to build an aqueduct into the city. Again the Jews protested, but this time Pilate had infiltrated troops in civilian dress into the crowd and on his signal they drew swords and randomly attacked the protestors, killing many of them.

Ashe opened another bookmarked volume.

In *On The Embassy of Gauis* the chronicler Philo, who died in 50 AD, described a later but similar incident to Josephus's in which Pilate antagonised the Jews by setting up gold-coated shields in Herod's Palace in Jerusalem. Philo wrote that the shields were set up 'not so much to honour Tiberius as to annoy the multitude'. The Jews protested first to Pilate and then to Tiberius, who 'wrote to Pilate with a host of reproaches and rebukes for his audacious violation of precedent and bade him at once take down the shields and have them transferred from the capital to Caesarea.'

According to Philo, Pilate exhibited 'vindictiveness and a furious temper', and was 'naturally inflexible, a blend of self-will and relentlessness'. What Pilate feared most was that in their reports the Jews would 'expose the rest of his conduct as governor by stating in full the briberies, the insults, the robberies, the outrages and wanton injuries, the executions without previous trial constantly repeated, and the ceaseless and supremely grievous cruelty'.

Pilate's prefecture ended in AD36 after he sent cavalry and heavily armed infantry to attack a group of Samaritans who were making a pilgrimage to view what they understood to be artefacts dating back to the days of Moses. According to Josephus, Pilate had the leaders executed. The Samaritans complained to Vitellus, Roman governor of Syria, who ordered Pilate to Rome to explain his actions to the emperor. And Pilate never returned.

'He was not, then, the sort of vacillating, reticent fellow solicitous of Jewish concerns to the extent of being prepared to crucify an innocent man in order to keep a few subservient priests happy. If he had found Jesus innocent – found no case against him, as most of the Gospels would have it that he did – he would have set the man free; if he found him guilty he had no alternative to sentencing him to death. In his ten years of governing the troubled territory there can have been few cases that were more simple: innocent, he goes free... guilty, he is crucified.'

It appeared to be a fact that, when he received no direct response to his questions, Pilate had Jesus flogged, which was a routine response under Roman jurisdiction, to encourage people to speak, but probably not a likely resort by a judge who considered the man before him to be innocent.

'And not for the first time,' continued Ashe, 'we are faced with the question: How did they know? It is quite possible that bits of the Jewish trials or interrogations were reported to the disciples by Joseph of Arimathea, or Nicodemus, who appear to have been both followers of Jesus and members of the Sanhedrin. But who reported the conversation and cross-examination by Pilate of Jesus? Certainly not the Jews, who were forbidden to enter the court house during a festival. So do we believe that Pilate stepped outside and said to the priests: "Okay, chaps, let me tell you how it's going, and what is happening in there, and the way I'm thinking"...? I suspect not.'

Pilate, the only man who could have sent Roman soldiers to arrest Jesus, apparently waited until the following morning to ask 'what evil has he done?'... Then he told the Jews: 'I find no case against him'. He found Jesus 'not guilty of any of your charges' and asked the priests again: 'What evil has he done?'

But somehow, said Ashe, the followers of Jesus were privy to the thoughts of Pilate while he was deliberating. And at some stage he must have mentioned that he had received a note from his wife about a dream she'd had the previous night.

According to the Gospel writers Pilate, frustrated, eventually handed him over to the Jews and told them to crucify him themselves. More confusion there, because crucifixion was a Roman punishment, not a Jewish one. If the Jews had found him guilty of blasphemy, they would have had him stoned to death – the same punishment as for adultery.

Then Pilate washed his hands – literally – of the whole affair, saying that he was 'innocent of this man's blood'.

'The formal washing of hands, incidentally, was a purely Jewish – certainly not a Roman – ritual,' said Ashe. 'I suppose it is remotely possible that, knowing this, it was a sarcastic gesture on Pilate's part. But more likely it is just another bit of descriptive writing added later in an attempt to emphasise a point. And it sits strangely with the reports that he then allowed his soldiers to mock and abuse and scourge the prisoner, to garb him in fancy dress as a king, complete with a crown of thorns… and then to lead him to his execution on the cross.'

In the meantime there had arisen a slight complication when somebody – the Gospels are unclear about who it was – mentioned the custom of releasing a prisoner to mark Passover.

Ashe said it was surely impossible for the Jews to have had any Roman tradition, and equally for Pilate to have felt the need to find a way of relaxing his emperor's laws in order to mark a Jewish feast.

'In fact there is no recorded precedent, either in Jewish or Roman law, for such a concession or practice. But, because the Bible tells us it was so, let's examine it, even briefly.'

If such a rule existed, the simplest course by far would have been for Pilate to have released the man he thought was innocent. It would clearly be against what was known about his character for him to have asked the Jews to nominate the prisoner of their choice.

But, if the priests wanted Pilate to release anybody, they surely wouldn't have nominated a murderer, a rebel against the Roman state, who was awaiting the ultimate penalty on death row – there must have been plenty of people in the cells who were more deserving of a governor's pardon on a feast day.

In any case, if Pilate considered Jesus to be guilty

he could not possibly have released him; and if he considered Jesus to be innocent he would be releasing him anyway.

Mark said Barabbas 'was in prison with the rebels who had committed murder during the insurrection'. He doesn't say what the insurrection was (except to imply that it was some form of rebellion, presumably against Rome) or who was killed, which presumably means that the event was sufficiently well known for people to recognize what event he was talking about. It must also have been a fairly recent occurrence for, if the trial and crucifixion of Jesus is any guide, judgment was swift in Pilate's courts. *John*, on the other hand, omitted any mention of deaths and described Barabbas merely as a *lestes* – the description we have come across before – which different versions of the Bible translate into English as brigand or robber, or simply a wrong-doer.

'But we know – or the Gospel writers knew – that the crowd outside the court was calling for the release of Barabbas. Only *Matthew* reports his full name... Jesus Barabbas. The full name was in the earlier editions of the other Gospels, but was removed by scribes who obviously thought it inappropriate or embarrassing. Leaving it in the *Matthew* version was therefore probably an oversight.'

Time for a pause for reflection, said Ashe. 'A few days earlier, thousands of people had welcomed Jesus into Jerusalem as their long-awaited messiah. Now the crowd – what the Bible would quaintly describe as the multitude – was calling for the release of Jesus Barabbas. And how does the name Barabbas translate...? *Bar* means son of; *Abbas* means the father… Think about that for a moment and we'll take a break: who was the Son of the Father?'

He said they should go for a dip in the pool, telling Shilling: 'You can swim in those shorts. They will be dry again within minutes.'

The pool at Ashe's home had been designed alongside the gazebo so that all day half of it was in the sunshine and half of it in the shade. Either that, or the gazebo had been built in that position for that reason. You had to look at everything in at least two possible ways, thought Shilling. The water was warm in the sunshine, so he moved into the shade where it was not particularly cool, but sharper and more refreshing. Vanessa appeared, pulled her shirt off over her head to reveal a bikini-clad athletic figure, dived in and swam half a dozen furious laps under water.

Ashe stood, glass in hand, in the shallow end, occasionally bending his legs to submerge his entire body to the top of his white-crowned head, the wine held high above him, reminding Shilling of the Statue of Liberty.

'I've been thinking…'

'Ah, good.'

'About the cross.'

'If more Christians would do the same, the world might be a better place.'

'I mean… thousands – no: millions – of people

hang a cross around their necks to honour Jesus. Yet it is a reminder of his agony and his excruciating death. So, is it the right thing to do, do you think?'

'Don't you think that the point of it is just that? That if anybody ever gives the cross at their throat a second thought, and I doubt whether many of them ever do, it is exactly for that reason: to remind them how Christ suffered for their sins.'

'That's not quite what I meant,' said Shilling. 'What I was wondering is whether Jesus, if he returned to earth as some people believe he will, would be likely to be wearing a crucifix.'

'That's a bloody good subject for a debate,' said Ashe. 'Would Jesus wear a crucifix? It's the sort of question one would like to ask the Pope who is, after all, the Vicar of Christ.'

Vanessa asked how their drinks were doing and, since neither of them could remember, said that she would go and check. Ashe took a gaily coloured beach towel from a pile and threw it towards Shilling as he climbed up the steps of the pool. 'The sun is less vicious now. Let's stay outside for a while.'

Vanessa emerged from the house with a new bottle in a cooler, a pair of fresh glasses, and the leftovers from lunch which she put on a table between them, before returning to the pool.

As a matter of history, said Ashe, continuing his lecture, the story of Barabbas had originally appeared only in the version by *Mark*. It was added to the others, he said, probably because it was too good a tale to leave out.

There was no record of the man Barabbas actually being released, nor – as you might have expected, given the nature of the New Testament, any account of what happened to him afterwards, such as his immediate conversion to become a follower of Jesus, in light of his miraculous escape. Nor was there any suggestion that the men on either side of Jesus at the crucifixion were colleagues of Barabbas.

'So what was this unexplained recent insurrection, which probably involved some injury and may or may not have involved an actual death? Could it, perchance, have been the massive disturbance of the money-changers in the temple precincts where, according to *John*, Jesus was wielding a lash? Civil unrest was precisely what Pilate was appointed to prevent.'

In leading a movement for a new – and obviously non-occupied – era for Jewish governance (and there were many such factions at the time), said Ashe, Jesus was effectively a Palestinian Liberationist: a freedom fighter.

'Jesus... the PLO guy...?'

'There are some who say that the disciples were a bunch of tough hombres. That he renamed Simon not as Peter the Rock, but effectively as Rocky. That Judas Iscariot meant Judas of the Sicarii, the knife carriers. And then there was Simon the Zealot, from a tradition fighting for the end of Roman rule. James and John shared the family nickname of Bar-Jona, which translates as Sons of Thunder. Fanciful? Well, it doesn't exactly fit with the idea of turning the other cheek...'

On the other hand, according to *Luke*, during the Last Supper Jesus had said to them:

But now if you have a purse, take it, and also a bag; and if you don't have a sword, sell your cloak and buy one.

'This, remember, is Gentle Jesus Meek And Mild. And apparently Peter, at least, did just that. That would easily explain why Jesus Bar-Abbas was a leader of rebels.'

The bottom line was that, if there was no Barabbas, *Mark* needed to invent one. If thousands of people, perhaps tens of thousands, were surrounding the court and calling for the release of 'Bar-Abbas', Son of the Father, it was a detail that would be remembered and probably should not be overlooked. So *Mark* needed to concoct some explanation for it. Pilate, according to *Mark,* had judged Jesus innocent and was emerging as something of a fan. But if Pilate was the good guy, how was it that Jesus was sentenced to die on the cross?'

The simple answer was to blame it on the Jews. Hence the invented tradition of releasing a prisoner, hence the appearance of Barabbas into the plot, hence the explanation for the multitude calling for the release of Jesus Barabbas.

'I promised that I would come eventually to the evil bit... *Matthew* took it one stage further, and when Pilate asked the crowd whether they really wanted him to crucify their king, *all the people answered and said, His blood be upon us and on our children.*

'It doesn't sound much like the sort of slogan that

would slip easily from the tongues of a multitude of people, does it? It isn't exactly easy, like *Romans Go Home,* is it?

'Consider this, if the story was pure concoction by *Matthew* it is one of the most evil sentences of all time. The interpretation is that the Jewish people are permanently guilty and condemned in the eyes of God for the murder of Jesus. As such, the cry of "His blood be upon us" means that the Jewish crowd in Jerusalem admitted full guilt for killing Christ and thereby invoked God's curse upon themselves and their descendants until the end of time.

'The words first surfaced in the early texts in the second century AD. They had become universally accepted by the Middle Ages. The result, among other things, was the terrible accusation that all Jews were Christ-killers and that Pilate was totally exonerated.

'Sadly, this is still a widespread belief in the Church today.

'*Mark* had allowed Pilate a modicum of blame in that, despite his personal feelings he had allowed himself to be coerced into going ahead with the crucifixion. *Matthew,* however, absolved him of all responsibility – it was the Jews alone what done it.'

And how, asked Ashe, might all this have come about? 'Simple. The first Christians were preaching to and trying to convert the Romans. It would be less than helpful if they, even in the person of one man, Pilate, were considered to be responsible for the Saviour's death. They needed another culprit, and the Jews were sitting ducks.

'It became known as the Blood Curse. And when it was published Christians – so called – started attacking Jews and burning their books and accusing them, generally as a race, of killing Christ. In the twelfth century the anti-Jewish programme was formalised into what became known as the Inquisition. It officially ended as recently as 1860, but it was an excuse used by the Nazis in the 1930s and it continues today with eleven cardinals running what is known as the Congregation of the Doctrine of the Faith.'

Shilling, thinking that he ought to make an occasional contribution, even if only to signal that he was still paying attention, cleared his throat:

'But Jesus wasn't a Christian, he was a Jew.'

'Try telling that to the Christians,' said Ashe. 'And try telling Catholics that the Virgin Mary was a Jewess.'

When Vanessa had said that he was on something of a hobby horse, she had been right. 'I had often wondered about the Jesus-Barabbas confusion, and whether Pilate could actually have appeared before the crowd and asked whether they wanted him to free Jesus the son of god, or Jesus the son of god the father. And also, what might have motivated him to want to release anybody at all.'

But historians looked for provenance just as policemen looked for corroboration of witness statements.

And it was all there, he said, '...in your little scrap of papyrus'.

The Romans didn't paste up wanted posters all

over town, partly because most of the population couldn't read, so there would be no point in doing it. Instead they issued hand-written documents detailing the charge and usually the description of the accused and handed them out to people who could read, and who could pass it on orally to those who couldn't.

This was effectively also the arrest warrant.

According to *John* it was the priests – the Jews, again! – who had issued the warrant. It may well be that the priests copied it out, because they were the Aramaic scribes, and it may even be that their staff distributed it, on the grounds that they were most likely to know who among the population would be capable of reading it. However what we also knew, said Ashe, was that, first, the Sanhedrin did not issue warrants, and second, that the Romans did.

'As for provenance... well... happily we know of somebody else who saw the warrant and read it. Josephus had a copy, and quoted part of it in his history. It was well known, at least in some quarters; the more memorable bits being the description of shortness and the stooped back.'

Ashe thumbed another bookmark but didn't read from it. Instead he said: 'You might think that the crooked back would have explained the lack of height, and that toiling over a carpenter's bench for twenty years or so might have been a fairly honourable explanation for a stoop – and incidentally by my calculation Jesus would have been middle-aged for those days, around forty. But the Christian scribes and translators wouldn't have it and deleted the reference from Josephus. Conveniently for historians they failed to delete it in one edition, the Slavonic version. And there it remains, although he doesn't quote his source. But it's virtually the same wording, the same document, that you now have. So it is reasonable to assume that it was Josephus' source.'

It was a failing, and to many a disappointment, that the Gospels did not include anywhere a description of Jesus, the man. 'You could argue that his appearance didn't matter and that only his teachings were important. But the answer is that none of them had ever seen him, so they didn't have the foggiest idea. Nevertheless, they must have wondered about it, and possibly asked people, but perhaps they did not like the answer.'

Luke – who incidentally was one of those witnesses who never set foot in the Holy Land – says that Zacchaeus, who 'was a chief tax collector and was wealthy', wanted to see who Jesus was, but *because he was short* he could not see him in the crowd. *So he ran ahead and climbed a sycamore-fig tree to see him, since Jesus was coming that way.*

'That may be a clue,' said Ashe, 'if it means that it was Jesus who was short. And so might the original reference to "physician heal thyself" if people thought that Jesus could himself benefit from some healing assistance. But we simply don't know.'

'Are there still copies of the Slavonic Josephus in existence?'

'Certainly, under lock and key in private collections. And of course in the Vatican library.'

‘Which brings us to the question of what McAuliffe was doing with one of the original copies of the warrant,’ said Shilling.

'He is the victim in a murder case, remember.'

‘Indeed, which in turn brings us back irrevocably to that wonderfully chivalrous band of Christian brethren, the Hospitaller Knights of St John of Jerusalem, Rhodes and Malta.’

Shilling could tell by now when Ashe was being sarcastic.

He refilled their glasses and made himself more comfortable in his chair.

Ten

When looking at history, said Ashe, it was important to remain aware that people living at – for example – the time of the Crusades, did not see themselves as existing in an era called the Middle Ages. They considered themselves, rather, as being at what we would call the forefront of technology; they assumed that just about everything that could be, or was going to be, invented to make their lives easier had been achieved.

They had developed saddles and reins for horses, and they had wheels on carts. But if they needed to travel from their village to a town they were not thinking how much easier it would be if there was a bus service.

After years of persecution, Christianity had been adopted as the state religion of the Roman Empire in 313, and in 380 was declared the sole religion, and it more or less spread from there, as the Empire had done years earlier. Eventually some eager believers decided that a pilgrimage to the Holy Land, to see where it all happened, would be an appropriate thing to organise, but the only means of transport known to them was the horse. They were not thinking how much easier it would be if there were trains and coaches and aeroplanes: the horse – or horses, because they would need a galloper plus a heavy pack horse for their luggage – was the modern and seemingly most efficient way to do it.

Sensibly, they usually travelled in groups for safety, and because there was as much danger from robbers in Christian Europe as elsewhere, they would be heavily armed. In the early days the Christian pilgrims were unmolested by the Jews and Arabs of the Holy Land as they sought out the 'cave' where Jesus had been born, the rock on which he had been crucified, and the tomb from which he had risen from the dead. Just like modern tourists, where they could they collected artefacts to bring home as souvenirs.

In fact there can't have been much left. As early as 326 Queen Helena, mother of Constantine the Great, had made one of the first pilgrimages and had identified – mainly wrongly – the important sites of the life of Jesus and brought back everything she could lay her hands on that might be considered a holy relic. Magically, she even managed to identify the very cross on which Jesus had been crucified some three hundred years earlier. And it was probably safe to assume that local entrepreneurs were willing to turn up further relics for the visiting pilgrims to take home and worship.

'A woman truly divinely inspired, was Helena; she had even ventured into Egypt and identified the site of the Burning Bush.'

As Mohammadism spread the Moslems continued to allow the presence of a Christian church in Jerusalem and all was relatively well until the Turkish Moslems took over and started harassing the pilgrims. Worse, they took to slaughtering Christians on sight.

Thus, in 1095, Pope Urban II called upon Christian knights and noblemen to win back the Holy Land for Christianity, promising a guaranteed place in heaven for everybody who took part. Now more than ever the pilgrims needed protection and this appeared in two forms – the Hospitallers, who ran the lodging stations and the hospitals along the route, and the Templars, knights of the Temple, who protected the travellers and fought the battles. Reports vary, but there may have been 100,000 participants in the first Crusade. It captured Jerusalem and also incidentally discovered what was claimed to be the Holy Lance – used for piercing the side of Jesus as he hung on the cross. They also claimed to have found slivers of the True Cross that had somehow been overlooked by Queen Helena.

They held the city for only 88 years, after which largely due to the great Arab leader Saladin it returned to and remained in Moslem hands. There were eight crusades in all. Perhaps interestingly there was less information about the later crusades than about the earlier ones. Maybe they had lost their appeal to historians. In 1291 the Knights lost Acre, and retreated with their tails between their legs.

The Hospitallers wandered around the Mediterranean for a few hundred years thereafter, fetching up in Cyprus, Rhodes and Sicily before eventually being offered a home in Malta. The Templars had set up in France, where they were disbanded in 1307 by Philip IV.

The selective memory of the Maltese, Ashe

continued, totally ignored the fact that the relationship between them and the Knights was never a comfortable one. One hundred years earlier they had organised a sort of whip-round and raised 30,000 florins to buy their islands from their owner, who in those days was King Alfonso of Aragon. Now, without any consultation, King Charles V of Spain had leased them to the Knights for the insulting 'rent' of a falcon, to be presented to the Viceroy of Sicily on All Saints Day every year.

The Knights were not even sure that they wanted the place. Since quitting the Holy Land they had become a navy, rather than a land army, boosting their already considerable wealth by acts of piracy against any ship not flying a Christian flag. In addition to plunder, they gathered slaves, some of whom they ransomed, some they kept and some they sold. They sent people to investigate the facilities of the three Maltese islands and were alarmed to discover that although there was an excellent natural harbour, there were no trees to provide the raw materials for building ships, nor was there sufficient soil to plant any. The 12,000 inhabitants lived in miserable poverty and spoke a hitherto unknown Moorish language.

After considerable argument among themselves, they reluctantly accepted the Spanish king's offer. Basically, they had nowhere else to go. They ruled the islands, generally treating the natives with contempt, for just over a quarter of a century – in fact until Napoleon arrived, wanting a harbour en route to Egypt, and the Knights surrendered to the French fleet without a fight. Although it must be said that in 1565 they had put up a remarkably heroic four-month stance against the Turks in what became known (in Malta, but overlooked everywhere else) as the Siege of Malta.

'So the Knights were on the move again. And again we come back to the important bit of the story, for our requirements,' said Ashe.

'Every time the Knights were kicked out of a place they were allowed to take their belongings with them. In most cases – but not by the French – they were even permitted to carry away their weapons. The vital element, though, is that they maintained possession of their religious keepsakes. Even the French, although if an icon was in a jewelled casket or a golden frame they would confiscate the valuable parts, had no interest in the relics, icons and other souvenirs.'

Von Hompesch, the last Grand Master of the Maltese era, had been allowed to take a so-called miraculous image of Our Lady of Philermos (after it had been removed from its frame) and his piece of the True Cross. Other Knights sailed away with relics including what was claimed to be the arm of John the Baptist. But a number of other treasures, and all the archives and paperwork, were abandoned in Malta. And there many of them remained to this day.

'I would guess – wouldn't you? – that the Jesus warrant was one of the Holy Land souvenirs that they abandoned,' said Ashe. 'That's the only explanation I can offer for its being here in Malta.'

‘So you think McAuliffe stole it from the national archives? Or somebody earlier stole it and passed it down to him?’

‘No. What I think is that one of the Grand Masters – almost certainly Hompesch – handed it, maybe for safe keeping, to his Masonic lodge. Although the Maltese were not allowed to join the Knights, they were allowed to join the Freemasons, an organisation that they had brought with them from Rhodes.

'Despite his reputation for cowardice in surrendering the islands, he had been the first Master who tried to ingratiate himself with the natives. He even took the trouble to learn the language and instead of travelling everywhere in a carriage with an escort he walked the streets, and would stop to speak to the locals in their own tongue. Although he liked dressing up in armour, he had never been a fighting man; he was a diplomat through and through, and until his ignoble surrender he was widely respected by the Maltese.’

‘That would explain why it was behind his portrait, I suppose,’ ventured Shilling.

‘Nowhere more appropriate,’ agreed Ashe. ‘On the other hand, it would not be an obvious place to look for it.’

‘Well, all that has been fascinating, Profs. It gives me a good background and a potentially reasonable provenance for my bit of papyrus. I have enjoyed the history lessons. But now I have to press on... I’ve got a murder to investigate.’

He thanked Ashe for his kindness and hospitality, then found Vanessa on the terrace and thanked her, too. She told him that if he was doing nothing, later in the evening, he'd find her on the balcony of the Gleneagles pub, where she went on a Sunday for what she described as the joy of watching the weekending Maltese leave her adopted island.

She had already explained that the economy of Gozo couldn't survive, even in the tourist season, without the reliable contribution of the Maltese.

It was just that the two groups of islanders didn't much care for each other.

Eleven

Chief Superintendant Leo Dillon didn't take weekends off. He argued that since criminals didn't stop work on Friday nights, nor should detectives. More importantly, working on Saturday and Sunday meant that, crime permitting, he was entitled to time off midweek, so he could play golf when the courses around London were comparatively less busy, and the green fees were cheaper. So Shilling knew that his boss would be at his desk when he called late on Sunday afternoon.

'I don't need one of those phones with a TV screen. I can see you from here, sitting by the pool surrounded by bronze bikini-clad beauties and a glass in your hand with one of those little tissue-paper umbrellas sticking out the top.'

'Close,' said Shilling. 'I am actually on the balcony of my hotel with a view across the Med into a beautiful turquoise blue lagoon. The sun is shining, the sea temperature is hotter than the air temp in London, and I'm drinking a cold lager.'

Shilling had checked in on Thursday, the day after his arrival, simply to report the findings of the autopsy. On Friday he had sent back by courier an envelope containing information about terrorist arms buyers.

'I nearly sent you a herogram after getting your package. They acted on it straight away. They even made a couple of arrests last night. Imagine that –

you got the old sneakies working on a weekend. That must be the first time in years they've put their boots on, on a Saturday.'

'A herogram would have been nice. It's always good to know one's work is appreciated.'

'You already have your reward. You're sitting in the sunshine, doing sod all.'

'Sitting... and trying to sift the possible suspects. It's a long list.'

'Well, the suspects are hardly your problem, provided that none of them is from here. You have no jurisdiction; you can't make arrests; all you're there for is to make sure that nothing that's happened bounces back to Blighty and that the murder of a Brit is being realistically investigated. How far have they got, the Maltesers?'

'I think we can discount the arms trade. To the dealers he must have been a pretty good customer. And to the end-users he'd be a fairly reliable and, for obvious reasons, a discreet source. There were Arab and African countries who he charged for work he didn't do... but, well, I guess they must be used to that. So I'm thinking it must have something to do with the money-laundering.'

'But it's the same as the arms dealing, isn't it? When you launder money you do the deal in advance. You know what the exchange rate is. The launderer sets his commission and the money man agrees to pay it. Where's the motive for murder in that?'

'I don't know, but the money goes in all directions: out of Malta in old Maltese lira and euros, in and out of most European capitals, even the Vatican. It's millions, maybe billions. If he was creaming off just one per cent, it amounts to millions in commission...'

'If the Vatican's involved, we know from previous experience that they are not averse to bumping off their bankers or their competitors. There was the case of the guy called Calvi, found hanging under Blackfriars Bridge in 1982. He was called God's Banker. I worked on that one. So did your dad.'

'I also think there may be a connection with the Freemasons, somewhere, but I haven't found what it is, yet.'

'Jesus! Spare me from the Masons! The Masons and the Met are an explosive mixture. We still haven't cleared them out of the hierarchy in this building. You never know who you're talking to, here. You're quite close to Sicily – I looked it up on a map – so can't you find a Mafia connection instead? Far better to focus on the bead-rattlers. Find the connection and we can shift it over to Interpol to investigate the left-footers. We have gained enough glory already on this one, just by uncovering the arms stuff.'

'Well, we are following up on the Masons. I don't have anything yet that links it to Rome.'

'How's your German? Ring the Pope and ask him about it. Do you want his number...?'

Shilling asked: 'Are you going to tell me it's Vat 69? The old ones are the best, guv! I haven't heard that one since I was at school.'

But he was thinking: Vatican... Vat 69... Vat...

Vatman. Eight o'clock... Plus a Maltese native who said he lived in Rome.

They concluded the telephone conversation with Dillon telling his subordinate not to work too hard and to remember the sun cream. Shilling put some shoes on and walked down the hill to the pub.

In London it usually required sixteen officers to follow a suspect efficiently and discreetly. And upwards of six cars, mostly black cabs. Galea told his superintendent that if the suspect had been Maltese, he'd need fewer cars because local drivers never looked in their mirrors. But a man from Rome, if he drove a car in the chaotic traffic of that city, would be spatially aware; he would know what the traffic was, and what it was doing, on all four sides of his vehicle; with a Roman on Gozo and Malta they would need to keep switching cars.

Galea's boss had immediately agreed to the suggestion of surveillance. A possible conspiracy charge – and conspiracy to murder, at that – sounded like proper policing. They were going through a quiet patch; they had arrested six teenagers crossing by ferry from Malta in possession of small quantities of drugs, and apart from routine surveillance on village squares at early mass that was the extent of it.

The backlog of criminal cases awaiting a hearing before magistrates stood at more than fifteen thousand. His arresting officers could be retired by the time the kids appeared in court, if they ever did.

'Bugger the budget! Get it organised. If Scotland

Yard thinks the evidence merits it, I'm not going to be the one who stands in their way. You'll need surveillance equipment – phone-tapping and external audio – get the magistrate to sign the paperwork for it. I'll send a car to Malta to pick up the gear. Choose the officers who'll know what they are doing. Sixteen extra shifts of overtime... *Il-Allah*! That'll keep the troops happy.'

Shilling found Loretto Pace sitting on the balcony of the pub, nursing the remains of a glass of white wine. He waved, pointed at the glass and stepped back into the comparative darkness of the bar to order drinks. While he was doing this, Vanessa and Mrs Field – Sarah – entered and he bought drinks for them: one more white wine and another pint of Cisk lager. The women followed him outside and he introduced them to his new acquaintance.

For a while they watched the traffic from the corner of the balcony. There were two marked lanes, yet the cars were somehow three abreast. Two policemen were struggling to keep the impatient motorists in some sort of order as they headed for the ferry to Malta.

'It's an interesting concept,' commented Shilling. 'The drivers wanting to turn left to the marina or the terminal are in the central lane; the ones going straight ahead for the ferry are on the left. So they have to cross each other to get where they're going.'

'That's Gozo,' said Vanessa. 'If there are two ways of doing something... To make things worse, a lot of the cars cutting across from the middle to turn left are not really going anywhere. They get in the queue just to make things more difficult for the Maltese. In the old days they used to come down to the harbour by foot and walk along the sea front in their Sunday clothes. They called it the *passagiata*. These days they do it by car: kids, granny, the whole family squashed in the back.'

'Why do they want to mess the Maltese about?'

'The two island races – and in spite of the proximity of the islands they are quite different people – simply don't get along with each other. They come over here for weekends and summer holidays, but they bring most of their supplies, food and drink, even gas bottles, with them because they think the Gozitans cheat them in the shops.'

'Do they do that?'

'Well, there are three prices for everything on Gozo: for locals, for tourists, and for the visiting Maltese – in ascending order.'

She told him that when a Maltese felt he had been overcharged, the shopkeeper might reply: 'Oh really? I am sorry. But I am only a Gozitan, you know. I am stupid!'

Pace said he thought Vanessa was exaggerating a little. But only a little.

Shilling told the women about the book that Pace was researching and they both expressed surprise about the extent of freemasonry on the islands.

Asked by Sarah to explain freemasonry to her Pace said that each individual lodge was ostensibly a charitable organisation. They were exclusive societies, he told her, each bound by oath to secrecy, which was presumably part of the attraction to members.

'What's the point of being in a secret society like that? If it's secret, presumably you can't tell anybody.'

Pace said he didn't know the answer to that.

They made small talk until Pace said he was heading back for dinner at the hotel and Shilling invited the women to join him at the restaurant Galea had taken him to; it was only about a hundred yards distant from the bar.

Over dinner Shilling learnt that Vanessa worked in Grasse, in the South of France, as a *parfumiere* and that in order to qualify she had been required to identify one hundred and forty-eight different scents. Sarah said she did public relations for the Israeli Institute of Technology.

The traffic had subsided by the time they finished their meal with coffee and a complimentary digestif of *Amaro Montenegro*. Shilling hadn't tasted it before, but enjoyed its refreshing herbal flavour.

'How are your taste buds?' asked Vanessa. 'Sip it carefully and tell me how many different ingredients you can identify. Dad used to make us do that. If we detected a new one we'd get a second glass.'

'Good game. Well, oranges, for a start...'

'But what sort of orange?'

'I don't know. Spanish? Israeli...?

'Don't be silly. It is Italian.'

'Sicilian, then?'

'Yes, but what sort of orange?'

'Isn't Sicilian sufficient?'

'No; it's blood orange. And it is actually tangerine. And it's the peel, not the fruit. What else...?'

'Honey or treacle...'

'Both.'

'Nutmeg? Coriander?'

'You're doing very well,' Vanessa told him. 'But there are about eighty more.'

While he continued to make guesses he occasionally caught Sarah's eye and she smiled; he thought it looked like a real smile rather than mere politeness. And her eyes twinkled or sparkled when she looked at him. He had heard of twinkling eyes, but wasn't sure that he had noticed any before that actually twinkled.

Sarah said they would give Shilling a lift back to the Grand: 'I know it isn't far, but it is all uphill.'

At the hotel entrance Vanessa also got out of the car. 'I can walk home from here,' she told Sarah. 'I'll stop and have a nightcap with Bob.'

He ordered black coffees and more Montenegro and they took their drinks out onto the terrace so that Shilling could have a cigarette.

'Sarah really fancies you. Did you notice? Wasn't she making it a bit obvious at the table? She asked me to put in a good word on her behalf.'

Shilling said he hadn't noticed.

'But what does it mean, when she fancies me? She wants me to invite her out for dinner? I just did that. She wants to have sex with me? When a bloke says he fancies a woman I think he usually means for sex.

Well... at least... I mean... I can only speak for myself...'

He knew that he fancied Sarah. She had what one of his colleagues at the Yard would often describe as 'breasts designed for maximum lactation'; she had a beautiful face and a smooth complexion and reminded him of a young Elizabeth Taylor. Vanessa, by comparison, was tall and lithe with legs that went all the way up and the sort of figure that was perfectly designed for a bikini.

Shilling already knew that he fancied them both.

'What she probably has in mind is dinner *à deux*, for a start. Who knows where it will go from there?'

'So, she fancies me and you don't...'

She put her hand on his bare arm. 'I didn't say I didn't fancy you. But she made first claim.'

'She's a married woman, though: Mrs Field.'

'Widow. Her husband was in the Israeli army, so was she. She was standing beside him when he was blown up. She watched him die. Met, married, widowed, all within a year.'

'How old is she now?'

'Same as me, thirty-six. Her father was – is – some sort of diplomat. She was educated in Israel to start with then when her dad was posted to the embassy in London she switched to school in England, which is how we met.'

'Thirty-six... So, she is still in the Reserve.'

'Yes she is. I think she still has to do a couple of weeks military service every year. I don't know what she does; presumably public relations like in her civilian life.'

She told him it wasn't necessary but he insisted on walking her home; he thought it was the proper thing to do and in any case that the walk would do him good. She lived only about half a mile away, along the upper coast road called *Zewwieqa*. It meant multi-coloured and presumably referred to the display of roadside flowers.

He took her hand. 'So, if you fancied me – dinner, just the two of us and then who knows? – why didn't you get your claim in first?'

She squeezed his hand. 'I know what you're thinking. Is she going to invite me in when we get to her house? But I'm not, if only because Dad is such a very light sleeper. Is she going to climb over this wall for a quickie in the bushes? And I'm not, if only because there are too many mosquitoes out at night.'

Nevertheless, when they reached the tall gates of her father's garden she kissed him deeply and passionately. When his hand dropped onto her breast she removed it, gently.

'First date,' she said. 'That's as far as we go. Thanks for a lovely evening and a super dinner. Now, go back to your hotel room and phone Sarah and ask for a date, and see where you go from there.'

The dining room was empty when he got back, so he assumed that Pace would have gone to bed. He called the lift but instead of going directly to his room he went down to the car park.

The silver Escort was parked there in a corner, unlocked because there had never been a car stolen on Gozo. There was a small collection of parking tickets on the front passenger seat. K-registration: hire car.

Shilling opened the door and looked at the names of the streets on which they had been issued. They meant nothing to him, and he didn't think he would remember them, so he stuffed them in his pocket in order to show them to Galea and check where Pace had been in the car, and compare them with the reports of the officers who were tailing him. He hadn't had a passenger.

And he probably wouldn't notice that the tickets were missing – at least, not until he collected another one.

PART TWO
Interlude

'...am I the only person here who is not privy to this Blood Secret?'

The cardinal sitting next to the red-faced diner who was asking the question said he didn't know the secret, either. Some of the others sitting round the table appeared equally at a loss. The convenor nodded to imply his understanding, and said it would be a good idea to order more drink. He summoned a waitress and called for more wine and more cognac.

When the door was closed again, instead of speaking he raised a questioning eyebrow at the man opposite, a former director of the Vatican archive, who slowly reached across the table, extracted a cigarette from the convenor's packet, picked up the lighter, held both for a few moments to give him time to think about what he was going to say, then popped the cigarette into his mouth and applied a flame to it.

'The late thirteenth century was a time of significant change for the Church,' he began. 'In the Holy Land the Crusades were starting to run out of steam and the knights were in complete disarray; in the rest of Christendom the Inquisition was in full spate.

'The knights had failed in their mission to capture and keep the city of Jerusalem and the two factions,

Templar and Hospitaller, had even started fighting, ambushing and killing each other's soldiers. They were doing nothing positive, except occasionally finding – or more likely buying – so-called relics or artefacts and sending them to Rome to be blessed and sold on to gullible bishops as genuine mementoes of Christ's life.'

'So many pieces of the One True Cross you could build a cathedral,' interrupted one of the cardinals.

'And although no nails were ever mentioned in the Gospels, enough of them to hold the slivers of wood together,' contributed another.

'Even the bones of the three wise men, now resting in Milan...'

'They found other things,' said the Archivist. 'The arm of John the Baptist... roses that had first sprung to life at the foot of the cross, when watered by the tears of Our Lord.... and most importantly of all a document, a piece of papyrus, dating from the time of the Passion. It was this document that the Master of the Knights brought with him when he sailed from the Holy Land and sought a private audience with the new Pope, Gregory X, in the summer of 1273.'

Nobody knew what was said during the meeting. But it was recorded by de Vertot and others that His Holiness and the Master were locked in closed session for eight full days. During that time the Pope refused even to see cardinals.

It was, however, on record that during or immediately following the audience Gregory offered the Hospitaller a cardinalcy, which he refused on the basis that it might interfere with his independence as a military commander, so he elevated his title from Master to Grandmaster with the equivalent rank of senior cardinal.

At the Council of Lyon the following year it was noted and it was recorded – and the manuscript was in the Vatican Library, number 4734 – that the new Grand Master took precedence over all the other cardinals, ambassadors, peers of France and other great lords who were in attendance.

Meanwhile the Pope had also ordered twelve galleys – three each from Pisa, Genoa, Marseille and Venice – to assist the Crusade in the Holy Land and borrowed or raised twenty-five thousand marks of silver to finance the campaign.

'I had mentioned the Inquisition,' the Archivist continued. 'At that time the Jews were reviled on three bases: first, they were simply different – different in religion, appearance and race; second, they had become established as money-lenders, and nobody – least of all the people who had borrowed their money and were required to pay it back – likes money-lenders.

'Worst of all, they were seen as the killers of Christ our Saviour, following the text in *Matthew*'s Gospel that they had called for the release of Barabbas and the crucifixion of Jesus with the words: *Let His blood be upon us and upon our children.*'

'It may be worthy of note,' interrupted the convenor, 'at least, I think it is worthy of note, that *Matthew* was the only Gospel to mention this call from the crowd. Yet the result was that the Jews were denied citizenship in most countries, they were persecuted, accused by superstition, and frequently tortured and burnt at the stake.'

'Back to the meeting between the Hospitaller and the Pope,' resumed the Archivist, nodding. 'In addition to showing great and unusual favours to the Knight, he issued a Papal Bull; his first. It instructed all bishops to quash rumours that Jews kidnapped Christian children and used their blood for making Passover bread.

'Incredible? But true. In the superstitious thirteenth century, whenever a Christian child went missing, as children sometimes did, and do, the Jews were blamed for it.

'This was the matter referred to in the Pope's first letter. He described the practice of accusing, trying and punishing Jews as "silly" and told the bishops to stop it, adding "...unless – which we do not believe – they be caught in the commission of the crime"!'

The convenor now took over. 'It was to have been the first step in a gradual process to end Christianity's virtual war against Judaism. But he didn't have time to pursue it because he died on his way back to Rome from his council in Lyon.

'And what caused this dramatic change of Church policy? Simple: it was the document that the Hospitaller Knight was so eager to show the Pope.

'Now, to answer the original question. The call by the Jews for the crucifixion of Our Lord was known as *The Blood Oath*...

'The Christian reaction to that call became known as *The Blood Curse*...

'Pope Gregory described the false accusation of Jews as *The Blood Libel...*

'The Blood Secret was the discovery that the Jews didn't call for the death of Jesus. They didn't arrest him. They didn't try him, and they didn't sentence him.'

'Who, then?' asked a bewildered cardinal.

'The Romans. Read your Gospels again. You'll find in *John* that Christ was arrested on warrant by a Tribune and a cohort of Roman soldiers and the following morning was brought for trial before Pilate. There was no need for any Jewish trial, but in any case it couldn't have happened at night, and it couldn't have happened at Passover.

'The document the Knight brought to Rome proved this conclusively. It was Pilate's warrant for the arrest of Jesus of Nazareth. In a word, it absolved the Jews from blame.'

It might be assumed that what the Pope saw was only a copy of the document, he said. Whether his gifts and actions were an inducement to the knights to part with the original, or a reward for keeping its existence secret, was and is unknown. But the result was that the newly promoted Grand Master kept the original, and he also kept the secret. Pope Gregory, on his behalf, kept a copy and shared knowledge of it only with the Prefect of the Inquisition.

'So it has continued; the Vatican kept the secret between its successive Prefects and Popes; the Knights passed it from Grand Master to Grand Master and they kept possession of it. As far as we know they still have possession of it. But the

Crusades fizzled out around that time, so that the first Grand Master in the Holy Land was also the last Grand Master in the Holy Land. The Knights Templar were disbanded in 1307 with many of their possessions being passed to the Hospitaller Knights who were effectively dissolved in 1798. Unless the document was destroyed or, being vegetation, has disintegrated through time, we need to find where it is now.

'We need to acquire it. If necessary we need to buy it. We may need assistance from the Vatican Bank to fund the expenses of the quest to find it, and perhaps much more funding for its purchase.'

He looked pointedly at a cardinal who was a director of the bank, officially known as the Institute for the Works of Religion, who nodded to signal that such support would not constitute a problem.

'And then,' said the red-faced cardinal, 'I suppose we need to decide what to do with it. I appreciate that it should certainly embarrass the new Pope. But if its existence becomes generally known it will embarrass the Church even more. It will show that every occupant of the Throne of St Peter has lied – even if only by omission – about what has been known as the Jewish Question. And with every Pope, in fact with every passing year since 1273, the deceit has been exacerbated.'

'If its existence embarrasses the new Pope sufficiently, that will serve our purpose,' the Convenor answered. 'The Vatican can work hard to improve its relationships with Israel and with Jews in general by way of making amends. The warrant can then be archived safely with the hundreds of other secret documents in our library, or maybe it will be considered most prudent to destroy it. We can decide when we retrieve it.'

Coffee was served. It was agreed that the Convenor, the Archivist and the Bank representative should organise the search for the document and report back when there was anything to report – hopefully it would be the simple fact that the warrant had been discovered and recovered.

When the bill was settled the Convenor telephoned his driver with instructions to round up the other six drivers and tell them to pick up their passengers from the front door of *l'Eau Vive*.

One

Loretto Pace's series of weekly lunchtime discussions had started by accident. After delivering a lecture on religious relics to students at the seminary, he had joined the table where a number of young priests were lunching and had been asked what a priest should say to a member of his congregation when asked a question to which he didn't know the answer.

The students could – and did – quote dozens of examples. Pace countered first by asking them how they would answer any such question if they asked it of themselves. Then he said that the answers were almost always there – somewhere – if they searched diligently.

They should read the Testament, and then read it again.

Where there appeared to be no possible, or logical, explanation they should not be sidetracked by what was considered to be 'science'... they should never forget the formidable force of faith, nor the power of prayer. And then there was the magical mystery of miracles: miracles sometimes happened.

In the event Pace was able to answer most of the students' questions, simply by quoting from the Bible which he told them he had read 'forwards, backwards and sideways', as he instructed them to do.

They had more questions for him the following

week. And eventually the lunchtime discussions became a regular event, finally moving into a small lecture theatre every Tuesday lunchtime. Now Pace would ask them the questions. He would also answer some of them and leave others for the students to ponder on and solve for themselves.

His current subject was the Resurrection. It was the belief in the Holy Land that a body started to decay three days after death, so by tradition certain practices were performed – invariably by the women of the deceased's family – within that time-frame to prevent it, or slow the process down.

Counting Friday as the first day, Sunday would be the third, and Sunday morning would be the time limit for this preparation or anointing of Christ's body with unguents and spices. Thus, according to *John*:

> *...on the first day of the week cometh Mary Magdalene early, while it was yet dark, unto the tomb...*

She and Mary the mother of James had followed the body from the crucifixion and seen where it had been entombed.

'A great stone or *gelal* – which in Aramaic means a stone too big for carrying, which therefore needed to be rolled – had been laid across the entrance to the tomb. So how did she intend to move it?'

Mary had no men with her, Pace continued. This was apparent because when she found the sepulchre empty she ran, presumably back into the city, to tell Peter and John:

> *They have taken away the Lord out of the tomb and we know not where they have laid him.*

'But she may have had other women with her; use of the word *we* could be the clue to that. *Matthew* says she was accompanied by "the other Mary"... according to *Mark* this was Mary the mother of James, and he says Salome the mother of the apostle John was also present. St *Luke* includes Joanna, the wife of Herod's steward, as being among the anointing party.'

Presumably Joseph of Arimathea and Nicodemus had been able to roll the stone into place. He asked: Would three or four women be confident that they would be able to roll it away? Apparently not, for *Mark* says that on their way down from the city the women –

were saying among themselves Who shall roll us away the stone from the door of the tomb?

'Let's pause there for a moment...'

Mark was the first Gospel written, he said; *Matthew* and *Luke* were next and *John* would have had all three versions in front of him when he was writing the fourth and last.

'If your mother had been present as a witness to the most historic event in the history of the world – to the actual rising of a man from the dead – the single moment that was absolutely crucial to Christianity, wouldn't you have mentioned it?'

He continued: 'And wouldn't you have been privy at some stage to a personalised eye-witness account of what the women actually saw in the tomb and in the garden...?'

It was not unusual for people to arrive late at Pace's meetings, nor for them to leave early, depending on their other mid-day appointments. But when a late-comer entered, Pace paused, recognising him as a cardinal, a man who had actually been one of the initiators of these lunch-time sessions.

Catching the speaker's eye the cardinal raised his head, signalling that he wished to speak to him.

Pace started to wind up his meeting:

'When she had left Jerusalem, probably in darkness, probably as soon as the city gates were opened, Mary Magdalene would have had no way of knowing that the chief priest had posted a guard on the sepulchre, nor that the stone had been sealed, probably with some sort of quick-drying mortar.

'But, in the event, the stone did not present a problem. When she, or she and her female companions, arrived in the garden the stone had already been moved and an angel (according to *Matthew*) was sitting on it. Or, says *Mark*, a young man in white was sitting inside on the right... Or two men in shining garments appeared and stood beside the women, according to *Luke*... Or it was two angels in white, one at either end of the tomb (and seen only by Mary Magdalene, after John and Peter had looked inside), if you follow the *John* Gospel....

'There was no sign of the temple guard.

'On his arrival John had found the tomb empty: no young man, no angels. The burial cloth – that would traditionally be eight feet of linen – was lying on a shelf. We don't know what became of that, except we can be fairly sure that it didn't find its way to Turin.

'So the more important question is this: who had

rolled the stone away? Think about it. We will discuss it further next week.'

The Cardinal told Pace it had not been his intention to curtail his dissertation; he had been listening with interest to what little he had heard of it. But he had a mission for the priest that was more important than his weekly discussion groups.

He explained the Blood Secret to him and Pace started to say: 'That all makes a lot of sense, because...'

But the cardinal held up his hand, palm outward, to silence him. 'We were aware that you would be able to follow the plot; that is one reason why you were chosen for this quest by no fewer than three cardinals.'

He added that the most likely place to find the document would be somewhere in Malta. This was Pace's homeland, which was the second reason why he was the obvious choice to search for it.

Money, continued the cardinal, should not be an obstacle. Pace should spend whatever was necessary to fulfil his mission. And when – not if – he found the warrant he should retrieve it, even if the only means of achieving this was to buy it.

'It is impossible, if anybody appreciates the political as well as the religious significance of this scrap of papyrus, to put a value on it. But you have the authority to spend up to a million to recover it; that is the sort of figure that we suspect would convince most people to part with it.'

'One million... what...?' asked Pace.

'Euros? Dollars?'

'Either.'

'Many people in Malta still calculate everything in Maltese lira.'

'In that case, euros, dollars or Maltese lira.'

One million lira would be 2.33 million euros.

'Are you sure about that...?'

The cardinal's expression clearly signalled that he could not remember the last time anybody had asked him whether he was sure about anything.

'Whatever is asked.'

The two men went over the details again so that the cardinal was totally satisfied that Pace understood both the mission and the importance of its success.

Then the cardinal said: 'By the way, the answer to your question today is to be found in the Gospel of the Hebrews...'

The crucifixion had occurred at the busiest time of the year for the temple guard. Jerusalem was full of people and they needed to be controlled. They would have worked late at night assisting the Roman soldiers in the arrest of Jesus. They would have been standing by in case of reaction by the populace to both the trial and the crucifixion. When, at short notice, they were given extra duties to guard the Holy Sepulchre they would have been totally exhausted.

'But it would have been a totally boring and monotonous task. Is it any surprise that, as *Matthew* reports, they fell asleep?

'And meanwhile, inside the tomb, Our Lord rose

from the dead. He later, as recorded in *Hebrews*, tells His brother James:

The Son of Man is risen from among them that sleep.

'So... He rolled it away, Himself. Or He commanded the stone to roll away. In either case, when the stone was moved the tomb was empty. A miracle.'

'Yes,' agreed Pace. 'If that is the answer that satisfies your own curiosity: a miracle.'

Two

Loretto Pace was a plodder; not a sprinter but a long-distance runner. He started his enquiries in the Vatican library reading everything he could find about the Knights – and especially about their treasures – from 1273 to the present day.

When he had eventually convinced himself that he knew as much as the archives had to offer he took the noon Alitalia flight to Malta and continued his research in the *Bibliotheca,* the National Library in Valletta. This building housed the personal libraries of the Knights but also all the archives and treasury manuscripts of the Hospitaller order.

There was no mention anywhere among the many lists of treasures of any piece of papyrus, nor of any document relating to the time of Christ. If it existed as one of their possessions they had clearly maintained their side of the Papal bargain and kept its existence a secret.

He turned to documents relating to the end of the Knights' Maltese era.

By the time the Napoleonic fleet sailed into Grand Harbour the Order was virtually bankrupt, financially as well as morally.

Their strutting arrogant existence had become an anachronism: no crusades to fight, no pilgrims to protect, no infidels to vanquish, no chivalry to exhibit.

The French revolution had nationalised 254 of the

Order's estates in that country, with a consequential severe loss of income.

In Malta the Knights kept both female slaves and concubines, sometimes three generations of women in one family. As monks their vow was one of celibacy, rather than of chastity: to a monk there was a wide and vital difference in definition.

As one historian, the Englishman Edward Gibbon, had put it: 'the Knights neglected to live, but were prepared to die, in the service of Christ.'

When von Hompesch, the last Grand Master of the Knights of Malta, surrendered Napoleon personally awarded him a pension for life and the ownership of a German principality. He was allowed to take with him a couple of treasures that had no intrinsic value, as far as the Emperor was concerned: the portrait of a saint... a fragment of the One True Cross.

Other Knights were permitted to carry away other treasures, including the relic that they claimed to be the arm of John the Baptist. Every item that was taken away was recorded, along with the name of the Knight who took it. Many of these items found their way to Russia when in desperation a small number of Knights elected the lunatic Czar Paul I as Grand Master.

Most of them were consequently lost, stolen or destroyed.

All the Order's documents were taken and stored in the Valletta archives that the Knights had constructed for that purpose, and there they were listed, annotated and described in detail.

Not one of them was described as being papyrus, nor as relating directly or indirectly to Christ.

Pace next turned his attentions to the last Grand Master himself. What did he know about him as a man? What were his interests? Was there any clue as to where he might have entrusted the safe-keeping of an ancient treasured single document?

He read everything he could find on the man, and there was a lot, including copies of the agreements he made with Bonaparte before sailing off into comfortable oblivion.

He was surprised to learn that von Hompesch had been a freemason; after all, what did the Knights, already members of an exclusive society, need with another club or organisation? Reading more deeply, he discovered that other Knights were members of different lodges, and then that the lodges had continued in Malta after the departure of the Knights.

He asked the helpful library assistant for documents relating to Maltese Masonry, and while he was waiting went out into the sunshine of Republic Square and sat in the shadow of a statue of Queen Victoria, while drinking coffee and kicking at pigeons pecking away at fallen crumbs around his feet.

Back at the library table he made a list of lodges that existed in 1798 and the names of the Knights who were members of them. Some of the lodges owned buildings in different parts of the island; who knew what secrets may be stored inside any of them?

The following day found him in a different archive – among the microfiches and bound volumes of back issues of *The Times of Malta*. This newspaper went back only to 1935, although there had briefly been earlier versions, variously known as *The Progress* and *The Sun*. But the papers had often run articles about the island history, including stories about freemasonry.

He made a note of the author of the most recent articles on the subject then used an in-house telephone to call the journalist and ask whether he had time for coffee and a short chat.

The man, name of Chetcuti, sounded happy at the excuse to get out of the office and even happier at Pace upgrading the invitation to lunch, and asking the reporter to nominate a restaurant. He suggested Da Pippo, a trattoria down a steep and narrow street opposite the Sapienza bookshop on Republic Street and therefore easy for a visitor to find. The journalist said that he would make the booking in order to secure a table.

Pace arrived early, gave the waiter the name of his guest and was shown to a corner table. Chetcuti was only a few minutes behind him. The waiter shook his hand and said: 'My lord...! Your guest has only just arrived,' and led him to the table.

Introductions over, Pace told the journalist that he was Maltese, now living and working in Italy and thinking of writing a book about freemasonry in Malta. Chetcuti seemed to be the obvious place to start, he said.

He had been impressed, not to say astonished, to

learn that there were as many as ten lodges on Catholic Malta.

'Ten... maybe more. There are, I think, nine official ones and at least a couple that are classed as irregular, meaning unofficial. These are lodges that were formerly accepted but in some way managed to contravene the rules and regulations so were banned. Nevertheless, they continue to operate as unofficial lodges. I could name at least two that come into that category.'

'But Freemasonry is a proscribed order,' said Pace. 'Our new Pope, when he was Prefect of the Doctrine of the Faith, issued an edict, ratified by the late Pope, saying that the faithful who enrol in Masonic associations are in a state of grave sin and may not receive Holy Communion.'

Chetcuti appeared surprised that anyone could quote the declaration verbatim but said: 'My friend, you have been away from this island so long that you have forgotten how it works! What we have here is not Roman Catholicism but Roman Hypocrisy... Ninety-six per cent Catholic, but only when it suits them. The rest of the time they totally ignore anything that doesn't suit them.'

He said: 'Whenever we run stories about the Masons there are anonymous phone calls suggesting that we might be in danger of losing advertising if we criticise the Order or even mention that it exists here. Happily, our bosses are above that sort of thing, but I think they may be serious threats. I have seen some lists of members of some of the lodges and there are top people among them – politicians, policemen, big businessmen (including some advertisers) even judges. There is no way of knowing who the others all are.'

After coffee Pace paid the bill and carefully placed the receipt in his wallet so that he could claim for reimbursement later. The two men walked together uphill and into the bookshop where the reporter pointed out a couple of books that might assist him with research. When they parted Chetcuti suggested that they meet again in a few days when he would bring him more of the information that he had gathered over the years.

Pace walked about the city until he spotted a cafe with shade and no pigeons. He asked for cappuccino and Kinnie – a local sweet but refreshing soft drink made from bitter *Chinotto* oranges and aromatic herbs.

Then he took the books out of a carrier bag and started to read.

The sun was below building height and Pace was on his second book and his fourth coffee when he found what he was looking for. It was a single line saying that before departing from Malta von Hompesch had made a farewell visit to his Masonic lodge.

He found Chetcuti's business card in his pocket and phoned him.

'You know von Hompesch...'

'I know who he was, yes.'

'Do you know which lodge...?

'Yes; St Joseph. It is now one of the irregular ones.'

'And do you happen to know who runs it... who is the Grand Master?'

'The Worshipful Master, they call it. It's a guy called McAuliffe, very well known on the island. Big wheeler-dealer.'

'Micallef...?'

'No: McAuliffe. He's British. Lives in a palace in Birgu. Where are you going with this?'

'Oh, nowhere, really. Just thinking.'

'Take care if you are thinking of approaching him. He is very well connected.'

'So am I,' said Pace to himself. To Chetcuti he just said 'Thanks,' and hung up the phone.

He walked back to archive of *The Times*, but it had closed for the day.

So next morning he was waiting for the doors to open and this time asking for everything they had on John McAuliffe, British businessman, long time established resident in Malta.

There were reams of it: he was involved with charities from the Red Cross to the SPCA, he advised governments at home and abroad, sponsored and supported organisations like Amnesty International and Greenpeace, mediated between Libya and countries in the west, negotiated with Arab terrorists for the release of hostages, and was a prime mover in bringing new businesses to the Maltese islands.

But there were also many references to investigations by the Maltese Treasury, the European Central Bank and the International Monetary Fund, mainly about the movement of money across borders. None of them ever amounted to anything positive – certainly there was no evidence of anything of a criminal nature.

Successive photographs showed him through several decades: as a young man with thick black hair to a pensioner with a shiny near-bald head and grey hair. He was broad at the shoulder, narrow at the waist. His nose was slightly crooked as though it might have been broken at some stage; he could have been a rugby player or a boxer in his youth. His age wasn't given but Pace correctly calculated that he must now be in his early eighties.

Something else that wasn't mentioned, anywhere, was freemasonry.

Pace paid for some photocopies and microfiche print-outs that he took back to his hotel to study and build a psychological assessment and a profile of the man. And another of von Hompesch. He needed to find the point where the two characters conjoined.

Three

It seemed obvious to Pace that, in agreeing to a bloodless surrender by the Knights of Malta, their first German Grand Master had not been intending to abdicate (he didn't resign until six months after Czar Paul had been elected in his stead). In fact he clearly saw the retreat not as capitulation but as a tactical withdrawal; he was a diplomat, not a warrior.

In any case the French knights, by far the largest in number among the Hospitallers, had had no stomach for the idea of fighting their own countrymen: at least fifty of them had even signed up to join the revolutionary army and had sailed on to Egypt with Napoleon.

The Hospitaller order had been forced to leave many other places – Jerusalem, Acre, Cyprus, Rhodes – and following each departure they had regrouped in greater strength. Now von Hompesch would have a principality and a pension and could use both as a base for a revival, a new order.

He also believed that his peaceful settlement would be looked upon favourably by the French who might even – and possibly sooner rather than later – permit the Knights to return amicably to Malta. The French wanted only the harbour, not the hinterland, which was worthless. They had no interest in the Knights' treasures or archives, which had no monetary value; they had not objected to his suggestion of leaving the bulk of them in the Valletta archive. He had been allowed to take a couple of personally cherished treasures with him; the important religious relics like the arm of St John would remain in the safe keeping of senior members of the conventual chapter, wherever they travelled.

It was a good job that they did; the gold, silver and jewellery that the French plundered from the Knights treasury had been stowed on board Napoleon's flagship *L'Orient* which was sunk by Nelson's fleet while at anchor in Aboukir Bay during the Battle of the Nile.

There would be only one relic, Pace calculated, that, like some special wine, would not travel well.

The fragment of papyrus was a fragile document, very nearly two thousand years old. It could not be folded; it should not be packed up in a saddlebag nor exposed to sea air and moisture on a voyage away from the island. At the same time, it was clearly far too precious to be stored as just another document in the archives.

There would be one place for it: with the Worshipful Master of his Masonic lodge. It made perfect sense to Pace; it was probably what he would have done, in von Hompesch's position.

Mad Czar Paul – when he wasn't donning his *magister* robes to flit between the bedrooms of his mistresses – also entertained the notion that as Grand Master he might reach an agreement with Napoleon and even styled himself 'Emperor of Malta' on the basis that his new Hospitaller titles included Prince of Malta. He would then take possession not only of the mid-Mediterranean archipelago, but also of the religious treasures and archives.

Pace thought it unlikely, however, that von Hompesch would have passed on any secrets to his Russian successor.

So the papyrus would remain, for eternity or at least for as long as it lasted, with von Hompesch's Masonic Lodge.

It was more difficult to get into the mind of John McAuliffe. There was a phrase somewhere in the back of his memory: What made Johnny run? Pace wasn't totally sure what it meant but it sounded appropriate.

What did the man need? What would tempt him? Not money, surely; he seemed to have plenty of that. Recognition, perhaps; but he had that, too; the photos showed him with American presidents and Commonwealth heads of government – and even, on John Paul's visit to Malta, alongside the Pope.

What about an honour, something akin to a knighthood? But the man was British and from what he'd heard about their honours system you needed to be either an upright citizen or a politician – or otherwise, like anywhere else, you simply bought one.

Maybe a Papal Knighthood, then.

It wasn't currently within his gift, but if the Vatican was prepared to spend millions of euros a knighthood would be a relatively cheap alternative although, from what Pace understood of the cardinals' plot, he might need to wait for a new Pope in order to receive it. On the other hand...

Perhaps he should simply appeal to the man's good nature, if he had one; his sense of right and wrong. A document relating to the death of Christ surely rightly belonged in the Vatican.

Pace thought that the answer would come to him when he met the man.

He drove his hired car to Birgu and parked outside the palazzo. The door was opened by the maid who told him that *sur* McAuliffe and his wife were in Gozo, and would be there all week. She gave him the telephone number so he could ring him.

'You need to clean the place, even when they are not here?'

Only in the mornings, she said, the windows were left open to allow air movement and prevent humidity and there was always a lot of dust.

Pace walked to a nearby cafe and bought a tuna salad sandwich in the local *ftira* bread and sat in his car eating it, and waiting for the maid to leave. Then he walked round the back and down a narrow lane until he came to a wooden gate in the high wall of the garden. It was locked, but the rusty fastening gave way when he leaned upon it.

The open windows were too high to reach, so he found a stone and smashed a small pane of glass in the back door, then put his hand inside and unlocked it.

He started at the top of the house. There was no obvious safe, nor anywhere to hide one. From what Pace had seen on television safes were normally set into the wall behind pictures, or in the skirting, or under a carpet. He took off his shoes and walked across the huge Arabian rug in the centre of the living room; if anything was underneath it, he thought that he would feel it.

There was nothing, so he lifted down each of the oil paintings, propping them on the floor against the wall. They revealed nothing except cobwebs; the maid obviously never dusted behind them. He checked all the drawers: nothing. Then he went back to the bedroom, climbed on a chair and looked on top of the wardrobe: still nothing. He spent two hours searching; the papyrus would fit inside a book so he removed all the volumes in the bookcase, looked at the top of the pages for any insertion, and replaced them.

There was no safe that he could see. Maybe there was a safe in the Gozo residence. Maybe McAuliffe took everything with him when he moved between homes. In any case, he was in Gozo and would either have the document with him or would know where it was.

Back outside, he rang the number. McAuliffe answered the phone. Pace said he was a representative of the Vatican and would like to meet him for a private discussion on a highly sensitive matter. He was given the address and directions for the house in Xaghra and told to come at eight o'clock: his wife would be out playing bridge, so they could talk discreetly.

McAuliffe reached for a pen and then made a note in the pocket diary on his desk to record a telephone call from a man from the Vatican, who would come at eight: *TF Vatman: 8.*

Pace had decided to play it straight. The two men exchanged small talk and McAuliffe poured them each a drink: eighteen-year-old Glenfiddich in gleaming crystal glasses. It would be unusual, anywhere in the Mediterranean, to get to the point of a meeting without exchanging a few irrelevant pleasantries.

When refills were being poured he mentioned the piece of papyrus. He was engaged on research for the Vatican Archive, he said, and there was a missing link; his research had led to the conclusion that a missing document was in the possession of the St Joseph Lodge. He would very much like to see it, he said.

McAuliffe was clearly surprised to learn the subject of their meeting. He had thought the sensitive purpose would most likely be one of banking and finance. It was almost as if he had forgotten that he even had the papyrus in his possession.

'How do you know that I – or we – actually have it?'

The question was all that was needed for Pace to be convinced that he had hit the target, bull's-eye. If the man had asked 'Why do you think...?' or 'Who told you that...?' it would be less conclusive. But Pace's speciality was in reasoning; 'How do you know...?' confirmed to him that what was under discussion was a fact.

'I'd like to see it,' he said.

'If it is a document dating back to the time of Our Lord you will appreciate that its rightful place is obviously in the Vatican archives.'

'Let's assume, because it is the assumption that you are making, that I have this papyrus that you describe; what rights do you think the Vatican might have to ownership of it?'

'It would be the most obvious place, wouldn't it, to house anything relating to the story of Our Saviour Jesus Christ?'

'And once in your archive it would never be seen again...'

'It isn't being seen, now. But it would help tell the story, help complete the story. Even today after two thousand years there are parts of it that we don't know, or are unsure about.'

Pace spread his arms in supplication, leaned his head to one side and smiled.

'Do you think I might at least see it?'

'I haven't said that I've got it.'

'But that would be unnecessary; I know that you have it. I'd just like to see it, if I may.'

'Then... let's accept that I have the thing that you are looking for. And you must accept that I am not going to give you sight of it.'

'We would... if it would help in some way... be prepared to recompense you for your trouble, and for any expenses incurred, in your safe-keeping of it...'

'Really? And how much do you think that might amount to? What is it worth, to you...?'

'Well... you or your Lodge have had it for a couple of hundred years and, supposing that you have maintained it in good condition, what do you think? A couple of hundred thousand?'

'Or a couple of million, maybe?'

McAuliffe had no idea of the value of the papyrus. He had shown it, once, to a lecturer at the University who specialised in the history of the Middle East. The academic had struggled to interpret the text but thought that it could be an ancient document like a piece of the Dead Sea Scrolls. It would however need to be subjected to carbon-dating, then to authenticating by experts, and then the owner would have to provide evidence of ownership – how it came into his possession, and proof, if he intended to sell it, that it was rightfully his to sell.

It had seemed to McAuliffe to require too much time-wasting effort.

But now that the Vatican had shown interest, and put money on the table, he thought that he should reconsider. Proving ownership would not be easy. He supposed that the rightful owners would be the Hospitallers, but the current organisation was far distant from the structure of the Knights at the time they had left Malta. In any case, there were such things as private auctions; some people would be prepared to bid for and to buy historic artefacts without being too particular about where they were buying them from.

If the Vatican wanted to join in the auction, they would be more than welcome to bid for it.

Pace told him that even a couple of million euros might not be out of the question.

'I was thinking in Maltese lira, as you must know many of us here still do...'

Pace shrugged. Nearly five million euros. He said: 'Even so...'

McAuliffe stood up behind his highly polished desk then crossed the room to a mirrored silver-topped table where the whisky stood. Passing Pace's chair he patted him on the shoulder.

'The Vatican has deep pockets,' he said.

He picked up the bottle and carried it back.

'More Fiddich,' he said, pouring yet another deep measure into the priest's glass and leaving the bottle on his desk in order to save another trek across the room.

Pace thought he would try a different reasoning tack.

'If you don't offer it, or sell it, to the Church what will you do with it? Forgive me, but you are not a young man. I believe you have no children to whom you might want to bequeath it. What will become of it when you eventually... pass?'

'You are quite right. I don't want it. I don't need it. Rightfully it should remain with my Lodge but that will give up the ghost when I do. I have no illusions; the brethren of St Joseph's Lodge are in it for what they can get out of it, which means what they can benefit from, mainly through my connections. Without me, there would be no Lodge.'

Pace sipped at his drink. From the little that he had been able to discover about the Lodge he believed McAuliffe was speaking the truth. The problem was that he was no longer sure about his judgement. He usually drank nothing stronger than white wine; he wasn't used to the effect of spirits served in the same portions as wine, and he was drinking the Scotch as he would drink wine, rather than sipping it.

All he was sure about, now, were the last words of the Cardinal. He had also patted him on the shoulder and told him: *'Don't come back without it.'*

'Tell you what...' McAuliffe was talking. 'Let's do the deal here and now. Fifteen million, and it's yours.'

Pace had no real idea of what a million was. He knew that television viewers of Papal elections were numbered in millions and that there were twelve hundred million baptised Catholics worldwide. Fifteen million was merely a figure that was fifteen times more difficult to understand than one million.

Nevertheless...

'I have no authority to offer such an amount. I can ask my superiors but...'

'Then, ask them.'

'I would need to see it, first. They will ask me whether I have seen it.'

'You pay seven and a half into my bank and you get to see it. Another similar amount and you get to keep it.'

'I doubt that they will part with any figure for something they, or at least I, haven't even seen.'

Pace didn't feel very well. He felt confused. The man was playing games with him, games that he couldn't follow. He quite clearly had the papyrus, and had it somewhere nearby, if not in Gozo then in Malta. He should tell him where it was. He must; he must tell him where it was and he must at least show it to him.

Don't come back without it.

McAuliffe was half turned away from Pace, reaching into a drawer for a tissue to wipe away a watermark made on the desk by his whisky glass.

Pace picked up the bottle by its neck and smashed it against the back of McAuliffe's head. The businessman tumbled out of his swivel chair and swivelled almost gracefully onto the rug.

Pace moved swiftly but slightly unsteadily around the desk. He lifted a wrist and felt for a pulse: it was there all right and throbbing fairly prominently. He put his hands under McAuliffe's armpits and lifted him, but every time he moved him towards the chair it revolved on its plinth. He put him down gently, then turned the chair on which he had been sitting so it faced the centre of the room, then dragged the body over the rug and up into a sitting position.

He was unsure what to do next, but thought that strapping him down would be the best option: the guy was going to be furious when he regained consciousness. On television he had seen people use parcel tape, but there was none in the desk drawers: only sellotape, which would be useless. In a room used mainly as an office he could not expect to find any rope. He took off his belt and tied down one of the man's arms, then he pulled McAuliffe's belt slowly and awkwardly through its loops and tied down the other arm. Both belts were sufficiently long to allow several turns around the arms.

It was only later that he noticed the curtain cord, which might have made the job easier.

The eyes opened slowly and stared blinking at Pace.

'Who are you? What the hell do you think you are doing? What do you want?'

The speech was slow, hesitant, slurred, as if the man was drunk.

'The papyrus... tell me where it is!'

'Papyrus? What's that...?'

Pace, unaware that the symptoms of concussion often included slurred speech and loss of immediate pre-injury memory, decided that the man in the chair was not only drunk, but still playing games.

Don't come back without it.

Colleagues would have described Pace as a gentle soul who wouldn't hurt a fly (the same expression was used in Maltese and in Italian). He decided he needed to force the information out of him. But how to apply pressure and persuasion? Was it possible to torture a person... gently?

McAuliffe's fingers were gripping the curled woodwork at the end of the chair arms. Pace prised the little finger of his right hand away and forced it backwards.

'The document... the papyrus... I want it... where is it?'

With each couple of words Pace pulled the little finger further back, against the joint. He wasn't totally sure what he was doing. He didn't want to hurt the man, but he wanted to threaten him; to show that he was being serious and was tired of being messed about.

'I... don't... know...!'

Pace hated what he was doing, and hated himself for doing it. But he couldn't image any alternative option.

'The papyrus...'

McAuliffe was sweating. His eyes were rolling; his chin was on his chest.

The eyes, steady for a moment, looked pleadingly at Pace, then closed.

'The papyrus...' He applied more pressure. There was a dull crack. McAuliffe cried out, briefly, then collapsed, and his entire body went limp. He was unconscious again.

Pace stepped back, moved to the desk and drank the remains of the whisky in his glass. He felt he needed it. When he recovered he'd ask him again. This time, aware of the pain that might be inflicted, he should be more co-operative.

He wiped his own brow with one of the tissues in the box on the desk and then loosened one of the belts slightly to feel for a pulse. This time there was none. He lifted one of the closed eyelids, not knowing exactly what he expected to learn from it but the eye was quite obviously lifeless.

Frantic, now, Pace felt for any sign of a pulse in the veins on McAuliffe's neck. Nothing: the Worshipful Master had gone to join whoever was his God: the supreme Mason, the Great Architect.

Pace sobered up pretty quickly and conducted a quick search of the building. He checked his watch; it was not yet ten o'clock and he thought it was unlikely that Mrs McAuliffe, who was playing bridge with friends, would be back much before eleven.

Upstairs he learnt that husband and wife had separate rooms – not unusual in a summer home in the middle of the Mediterranean where the heat of two people sharing a bed was considerably greater than the heat of a single occupant. There was nothing in the husband's bedroom.

Back on the ground floor he rolled up the carpets – the large rugs – then, finding no floor safe, rolled them back again. He removed all the paintings as he had done at the Birgu house, and he checked the books in the bookcase for insertions between the covers or among the pages. Again... there was nothing.

It was far more likely, he reckoned, that the papyrus would be in Birgu. If he left now he could get the ferry, drive back across the island and continue his search. The maid would not appear until morning.

At the front door he remembered something. He had seen American crime scene investigators on television and forensic scientists often found minute traces of blood or hair on items that had been used as weapons. He wasn't unduly worried about his fingerprints being found on the glass from which he had been drinking: first, his prints were not on record anywhere, not even in the Vatican; second, why shouldn't he have been at the house, enjoying a social drink?

But the Glenfiddich bottle was different. He went back to McAuliffe's desk and picked up the bottle and took it with him.

Crossing the Gozo Channel on his return to Malta he took a swig from it on the darkened sundeck and dropped it over the side of the ferry.

Three

Pace was sitting in his car outside the Birgu house on Tuesday morning when the police cars arrived. The body would have been discovered by the wife – the widow – late on Monday. On Tuesday, after he had been inside overnight for a second search, the maid would have reported the break-in, the broken window in the garden door and the displacement of pictures and maybe other factors. The uniformed police were followed by detectives, then scene-of-crime technicians in white paper overalls.

Wednesday morning found him walking along the tombstones of long-forgotten Knights that formed the paving of the central aisle of St John's co-cathedral (it shared the distinction with an earlier church in the former capital city, Mdina). He was watching the worshippers who waited for confession; the larger queue would be for the most tolerant and most easily forgiving priest.

Bless me father for I have sinned... He told the priest that he had unintentionally hurt a man and he had died as a result of the injury he had inflicted. He hadn't intended to hurt the man, only to prove his seriousness, but the man was eighty-three and seemingly died of a heart attack.

'Then you cannot know,' the priest told him. 'The man might have died in any case. Perhaps it was his time... So long as you did not have evil in your heart...'

Considerably elated, Pace went to a side chapel to see again one of his favourite paintings, *The Beheading of St John* commissioned by the Knights from Caravaggio. He had read that it had recently been restored. But he was alarmed when he realised that 'restored' meant recreated as new. The painting looked as if it had been finished yesterday with the oil still wet; he hated its newness.

Around mid-day the widow returned to her regular address and, once installed, was visited by a lot of people, presumably calling to express their condolences.

Pace watched with special interest, in case any of the callers left the house with a package that they hadn't brought with them. He was watching again on Thursday morning when two men – fairly obviously both detectives – arrived and entered the house. They had looked as if they were going to approach his car so he had driven away and continued his observation from a safe distance, his car parked out of sight down a side road.

He watched them leave, carrying bags of what appeared to be files and ledgers.

He followed their car, all the way through Malta to the ferry port at Cirkewwa, and across to Gozo.

Instead of heading for the police station in Victoria the two cops drove first to the Grand Hotel and took the bags of paperwork in with them. They spent about twenty minutes inside before coming out empty-handed, getting back into the car and heading towards Victoria.

Pace left them to it. He went in to reception and

booked himself into the last available room in the place.

Sitting in his car outside the palazzo in Birgu he had originally wondered whether the two visitors might be police officers who were members of McAuliffe's lodge, arriving to take charge of the treasure. The following day, seated alone in a corner of the hotel's street-level terrace, he heard the waiter address one of them as *Sur*-Inspector, so it confirmed that they were policemen: one Gozitan-local and the other foreign and therefore unlikely to be members of McAuliffe's lodge.

He had followed them to the Xaghra house, from where they had emerged carrying nothing. The following day he trailed Shilling into town and watched him enter an artists' supply shop then drop what appeared to be a framed picture on the back seat of his car.

Perhaps, he thought, he had retrieved the papyrus and decided to frame it. When Shilling left his car to go into the computer shop he thought he would go and check.

But as he moved towards the parked car a traffic warden appeared as if from nowhere and placed his motorcycle across the front of his car.

'I've only just arrived, and I will only be a minute,' Pace told him, in Maltese.

'Sorry: too late. I have already started to print the ticket.'

Pace took the ticket from him and tore it in half.

'Don't throw it on the ground or I will have to

give you another fine, for littering. You won't need the ticket; the penalty will be on your credit card bill with the hire-car company.' Then the warden moved to Shilling's car and printed out another one.

Pace followed Shilling by car to Xaghra again and then, on Saturday and again on Sunday, on foot to Ashe's house. But at reception he had noticed that he had arranged for a safe deposit box...

Their meeting on the balcony at Gleneagles had been pure coincidence – except that it was the nearest bar to the hotel and therefore it was frequented by a number of other guests.

He had been surprised to be asked about McAuliffe, but thought he had probably proved his professed lack of knowledge by introducing his hasty McAuliffe-Micallef diversion. But at least now he could justifiably raise the subject with the policeman at a future date.

He made a check call to the Cardinal on Sunday afternoon – about the same time that Shilling was making his report to Scotland Yard. Sunday was a normal working day for cardinals.

It went well enough until Pace mentioned a link with freemasonry.

'Oh no!' his boss had exclaimed. 'Keep those people at arm's length. Whenever we tangle with the Freemasons the Church seems to come out of it as second best!'

Four
It-Tnejn

After only a couple of days on Gozo Shilling was already thinking of the Gleneagles bar as his local, and he appeared to be treated as a regular. Entering the pub he'd get a beaming smile and a cheery *bonasira* from mine host; the young boy, Mario, would be reaching for a pint glass before Shilling had put in his order; and the fishermen gathered in the corner to bemoan in high decibels the dearth of fish in the Channel would nod or wave in acknowledgement.

There were more ex-pats on the balcony that evening, all of them retired and resident on the island: a former Charlotte Street ad-man, a Fleet Street journalist, a West End lawyer, an airline pilot, an IT specialist, a diplomat... all of them having decamped from the English capital's dreary winters and unreliable summers for the more stable and temperate climate of the Mediterranean.

They were talking about the death of John McAuliffe, a fellow Brit. He had been found dead exactly a week ago; the information had been released to the media on Tuesday but because the local television news was broadcast only in Maltese – a language that none of the Brits had managed to master – they had not learnt about it until Wednesday's English language papers came out.

On Thursday came the news that the police were

treating the death as suspicious: the first mention of murder was published on Friday. On Saturday the press bureau in Floriana revealed that Scotland Yard was 'assisting' in the investigation. Sunday's papers carried fulsome tributes from the great and the good about the beneficial effects of McAuliffe's contributions to Maltese life and the islands' economy.

Towards sunset on Monday evening his life and death were very much the hot topic of conversation.

The ad-man, who was married to a local, said that the word in the supermarkets and village stores was that it was a mafia assassination. The reporter said he thought that was 'a bit knee-jerk': anything that involved money and murder in Malta was automatically assumed to mean Mafia. And the lawyer chimed in to say that, these days, it could just as easily be Russian Mafia as Sicily's *cosa nostra* – there were a lot of Russians now living on Malta.

The pilot wondered why the murder hadn't been mentioned in the first reports and what the motives might have been; there had been no suggestion that anything had been stolen.

Shilling moved closer to the group in order to listen in on their conversation and they – recognising a fellow Brit – invited him to join them.

'Holiday?'

'Just visiting.'

'We're talking about the mysterious death of a British businessman, here on the island. Guy called McAuliffe. You heard about it?'

'It was in all the papers.'

By seven-thirty most of the men were leaving to meet or to be picked up by their wives and going on for dinner, mainly within a hundred yards or so of the bar. Only the journalist remained when the others left. He called up pints of Cisk for the two of them and asked: 'I know you, don't I?'

Shilling, too, had thought that the face looked vaguely familiar but had been unable to place it.

'You're "Little-Boys" Shilling's lad, aren't you? So I guess you must be the team of top detectives sent from the Yard as reinforcements...'

It was a while since anybody had referred to Shilling as anybody's lad, but he nodded.

In the early sixties TV comedian Benny Hill had sung a ditty about a wayward milkmaid who charged 'big fat men at two pounds ten and little boys a shilling...'

Almost overnight – certainly before the BBC had repeated the show – a nickname had been created (some said it was coined) for police cadet Andrew Shilling... A. Shilling had become 'Little-Boys A. Shilling' and then just Little-Boys.

He remembered, now, that he had met the reporter at his father's retirement party. Hacks and cops had enjoyed a good working relationship in those days; they ate together, went drinking together, entertained each other at home, god-fathered each other's children. They had all been mates, often swapping information; they worked on a basis of mutual trust. It was a different world in his dad's day. Bob Shilling couldn't imagine inviting any current Fleet Street people to his retirement when it came, even if Fleet Street existed, which it hadn't done since the mid-eighties.

'Not reinforcements. More like just a watching brief. You know the sort of thing, I'm sure.'

Cautious, he asked: 'You still putting pen to paper, are you?'

'Only when I am asked. Most of the people I worked with have gone off to the Great Newsroom; most of the rest, the young kids, don't remember me, so I don't get asked very often. I put a few pars round on friend McAuliffe, but most of them ignored it. His name isn't familiar in London and these days they are mainly interested in what they call celebs.'

'It's the same at the Yard,' Shilling told him. 'They will run a dawn raid for a well-known name, with all the full media circus. But they could just as easily invite the person to appear with his lawyer at a local nick and at a decent hour.'

He sipped his drink: 'Anyway, keep in touch with me on this one, if you like, when I get back. There may be a story in it for you. It won't come out, otherwise – certainly not from this end...'

The two men exchanged contact details and Shilling finished his pint and walked back up the hill to his hotel. He had a date later that evening with Sarah Field.

After showering and changing into a pair of long cotton trousers Shilling answered a knock on the door and found Loretto Pace standing there. He had visited the widow McAuliffe that morning, expressed his condolences and asked her about her husband's Lodge. She said she knew very little about Masonic business, but when he had mentioned von Hompesch she had remembered the portrait and the broken frame that the English policeman had taken away. He then remembered Shilling's visit to the art shop and picture-framer's: there was suddenly no doubt in his mind about the whereabouts of the missing piece of papyrus.

Now, standing in the hotel corridor, he told Shilling:

'I was hanging about on the terrace, hoping to catch you on your way in, but I missed you. I found out a bit more information about the man you were asking about, the Englishman McAuliffe, and his Lodge.'

Shilling invited him in and offered him a drink, which Pace declined.

'He was Worshipful Master of the St Joseph Lodge, which is one of the irregular lodges that I think I mentioned...'

'St Joseph the Worker?' Ashe had mentioned the saint's name to him as an excuse for extended holidays for 'the workers'.

'So you mean there were lodges for the great and the good and the rich and the mighty, and another lodge for the working class? How democratic!'

Pace smiled. 'Not at all. The feast day in honour of St Joseph the so-called Worker was an invention of the late Pope. It is celebrated on the first day of May, so that good Catholics could share the public holiday in honour of a Christian saint, rather than in recognition of a communist-inspired day off work.'

Personally, he said, he was unsure whether Joseph was literally 'a worker' in the normal understanding of the term.

'In the original Greek texts of *Matthew* Joseph the husband of the Blessed Virgin Mary was described as a *tekton*. The word translates as somebody who is involved in building development; it gives us the words architect and technology. I'm aware that it has been translated as carpenter, and Joseph would almost certainly have been skilled at that and other associated trades and crafts. But at the time of the birth of Our Saviour the town of Nazareth was being built. It is more than likely that Joseph was a developer, or one of the developers.'

Good grief, thought Shilling. Was there nothing in the Gospels that was correct, or correctly translated?

'So if Joseph wasn't actually a carpenter, it's unlikely that Jesus was one...?'

'We don't know. *Mark* says he was a *tekton* but a carpenter would be a *tekton* of wood; he could just as easily have been a stone-mason – a *tekton* of stone. But we might assume that He would have been taught the craft, or crafts.

'More importantly to the Masons, God was The Great Architect. That's why their symbolism includes a square and a compass – the basic tools of the profession. Joseph was a *tekton*, which can be translated as architect, so his name is highly appropriate as the name for a Masonic lodge.'

'What more do you know about McAuliffe's lodge?'

'Importantly, that the last Grand Master of the Knights on Malta, the German von Hompesch, was a member of it. But I think you already knew that...'

Yes, agreed Shilling; he told Pace he had discovered that for himself.

'And the Knights had left something – possibly more than one item – in the safe-keeping of the Lodge when they left the island. But, in particular, an ancient document, a small piece of papyrus, that I believe is now in your possession. I'd like to see it, if you would be so kind...'

'The best I can do...' Shilling stood and walked to the dressing table, opened a drawer and took out a piece of A4 copying paper... 'is to show you this.'

He handed the photocopy to Pace who stared at it in disbelief that he had come so close to achieving his goal. He didn't understand Aramaic; the hieroglyphics meant nothing to him.

'Do you know what it is, and what it says?'

'More or less. It is something like a warrant or maybe a wanted poster; it would have been handed out in the streets of Jerusalem. "If you know the whereabouts of this fellow, you are to inform the authorities" – that sort of thing. It is in Aramaic, apparently; not a language I speak, myself.'

'And the original...?'

'I am afraid that I don't have it.'

'...Because, as you will appreciate, it is rightly the property of the Vatican.'

Shilling smiled. 'How do you come to that conclusion?'

'It was... is... the property of the Knights of St

John, a holy order of monks. The order no longer exists in its original form, so its property becomes the property of the Church.'

'That's not my reading of it.' It occurred to Shilling that Pace might think he was referring to the reading of the papyrus, so he quickly corrected himself: 'It's not my understanding. The Knights may have been monks, of a sort, but as I understand the situation they were not in fact directly subject to Vatican rule. In any case, this was a piece of paper – effectively – that was handed out in the street; in which case it presumably belongs, if it belongs to anybody, to the person to whom it was given in Jerusalem, all those years ago. Or to their heirs, I suppose.'

'It is also a document relating to the life of our Saviour, Jesus Christ...'

'In which case, does it relate to the Jews, or to the Roman empire? It's a moot point. But the Roman Catholic Church didn't even exist at that time; it can hardly claim any ownership. In any case, it is all academic. I honestly don't...'

As Shilling was speaking Pace laid the photocopy on top of the printer, just inside the big double doors leading to the balcony. A gust of wind blew it off onto the carpet and Shilling bent down to retrieve it.

As he tried to slide a fingernail underneath the sheet of paper Pace tipped the photocopier off the table and on to Shilling's head.

He was unconscious, he thought, for probably thirty seconds; at least, no more than a minute. But when he recovered his senses he was strapped into a wooden chair. It all seemed familiar to him: the head injury, the trouser belts wound along and restraining each arm. He could see the evidence photographs in his mind.

Rule One – there were lots of rules in a policeman's book, and they were all Number One – was: never turn your back on a suspect.

What surprised him most, after his own stupidity, was that he was literally seeing stars – something he had thought happened only in children's cartoons; but multicoloured five-pointed stars were visibly encircling his head.

His head was pounding painfully as he looked around the room and saw the printer-copier lying upside down on the carpet.

'I think you ought to know that you are in serious trouble,' he told Pace. 'If you have damaged that printing machine... I had already arranged to sell it on, virtually as new...'

'The original document...'

'Told you: don't have it.'

Rule One about the restraint of prisoners is that you restrain all four limbs, or you stay behind them.

Pace didn't know the rule.

As he approached his chair Shilling kicked out, catching the man squarely in the crotch, hard, with his instep.

He watched as Pace's face lost all of its colour, then continued to watch as he vomited on the carpet.

'I hope you're not going to expect me to clean that up.'

Pace, lesson learnt, passed behind Shilling's chair and went into the bathroom. Shilling could hear running water as he presumably washed his face.

When he returned he reached over Shilling's shoulder and prised the little finger of his right hand that was tightly gripping the curled decoration at the end of the chair arm.

'Tell me... how is your heart?'

'What I have told you is that I don't have the original that you are looking for.'

'No... safe deposit box, I think.'

'No... Royal Mail... somewhere in England.'

Pace was breathing heavily as the pressure on Shilling's finger increased. As it came fully back, against the joint, the detective cried out in surprise as much as in pain. It was a loud 'Ow!'...

Very loud.

Shilling reckoned later that what happened next had taken about two seconds, but he watched it all in slow motion.

As he had cried out he had seen the handle of the hotel room door drop as it was being opened. He was aware of one figure coming in to the room at some speed, and two other shadowy figures standing in the doorway.

Pace, positioned slightly to the side of the chair and well out of the reach of Shilling's feet, had his back to the door and to them as the first person – Sarah Field – struck him with the side of her hand against his neck, just below the chin then as he spun round hit him again in the middle of the forehead. Pace crumpled to the floor in front of the chair.

Sarah bent down and placed her finger tips against the side of Pace's throat and waited for a few seconds.

'Shit!' she said. 'They always said I didn't know my own strength.'

At that point Shilling's memory and observation reverted to real time.

She motioned to the two men who had followed her in. They were both short, swarthy, curly haired and dressed alike, in blue shirts and dark blue trousers. They could have been policemen, in uniform, but Shilling recognised them as Israelis – out of uniform; Israelis in plain clothes all dressed the same way.

Sarah quickly unfastened the belts and Shilling took his own belt from her and threaded it back through the loops of his trousers.

'You okay?'

'I might – I mean he might – have broken my finger.' He looked at his right hand; it was throbbing and swollen at the joint. 'Anyway, it hurts a lot. And I've had a bit of a blow to the head... that photocopier, over there.'

One of the men opened the fridge door. 'No ice. Is there an ice machine on this floor?'

Shilling didn't know. He watched as the second man got a handful of toilet paper and tissue from the bathroom and started to clean up Pace's vomit.

'What are we going to do about Chummy, here?'

He was a policeman and he was confronted with a body and whatever offence had been committed he was an accessory, albeit an unwilling or uninvolved one. His thinking was totally contrary to that of a policeman: he was thinking that he, or they, needed to dispose of a body.

He looked at the two guys with Sarah. Leave it to them, he thought. They are probably used to doing it.

Sarah was going through Pace's trouser pockets. She found his wallet, opened it, studied his ID card then held up a set of car keys.

'Any idea where his car might be?'

'In the underground car park. Lift goes straight down there. It's a silver Escort.'

She tossed the keys to one of the men who caught them and dropped them into his own pocket.

She drew the curtains closed and turned on the lights.

'Getting dark,' she said, threading Pace's belt back on to his trousers. 'We can move him in a few minutes.'

'No you can't. There are cops outside. They've been following him.'

'You're a policeman. Can't you call them off?'

'I don't see how I can.'

He thought for a moment.

'The best I could do would be to invite them inside for a drink while your guys drive his car out – is that what you were thinking of doing?'

'Yes; but I'll have to clean you up a bit. You can't have a drink with policemen while you've got blood running from your head. And your hand... you'll need to keep it in your pocket all the time.'

'Let's do that, then.'

'You were due to be in the bar in any case,' she reminded him. 'We had a date to meet there. You were late. That's why I came up to the room.'

'I was otherwise detained. As you saw.'

'I guessed there must be a problem. Because in my experience Englishmen are never late for appointments. I was going to use the phone, but...'

She'd obviously had very little experience of Englishmen, thought Shilling. But her opinion had worked to his advantage: it had possibly saved him a couple of fractured fingers.

'And what about Santa's little helpers – your boys in blue? Were you planning to bring them along on our date? Where have they gone, by the way?'

Sarah had clearly been in charge. She had been instructing the two men, mostly without speaking, mainly by hand signal.

'One's gone to check that the car's there. The other is looking for ice for your hand.'

As if on cue one of them returned to the room with a full ice bucket.

He looked in the wardrobe, found a plastic laundry bag, emptied the ice into it and handed it to Shilling who stuck his right hand inside it.

She lifted the copier back onto the table and pressed the switch. It buzzed and rattled a bit, then settled into a steady hum. She pushed the print button. The machine hummed louder, then clicked a couple of times and a piece of plain paper appeared in the tray.

'Looks as if it's working. It must have had a soft landing, on your head.'

Sarah took Shilling's hand and led him into the bathroom where she bathed his head. She dried his hair with a hand towel and combed it gently.

'Perfectly presentable,' she told him.

'Now go downstairs and see whether you can divert the cops' attention from the car park for five or ten minutes.'

That turned out to be easy. The two officers were sitting, totally bored, in their car on the road outside the hotel's main entrance. When he leaned on the roof of the car the driver lowered his window.

'How's it going?'

'All quiet. He's gone upstairs for an early night.'

'We should do the same. Come inside and I'll buy you a drink.'

They appeared hesitant, but only momentarily. They left their car and followed the Scotland Yard man into the hotel bar.

Sarah, watching from reception, picked up a house phone and asked for Shilling's room.

Sitting on the terrace she could keep an eye on the men in the bar while watching two cars – one of them belonging to Pace – emerge from the car park. When they were out of sight she walked into the bar and kissed Shilling on the cheek in greeting.

'Sorry chaps,' he said. 'My date has arrived, I'm going for dinner. I wouldn't think there's a lot of point in your hanging about here tonight. Why not check in and ask whether you can go home?'

Sarah put her arm through his and they walked towards the lift.

'We're not going for dinner,' she told him.

'I'm taking you to the hospital.'

'Why? I'm fine, honestly.'

'Bang on the head, possible concussion. And more than likely a broken finger. More importantly, you'll have an alibi with the timing on official record.'

She drove him to the island's general hospital and told the receptionist:

'My friend slipped in his hotel room and pulled a computer printer down onto his head. And he hurt his finger when he hit the ground.'

He was made to lie on a trolley and taken for x-rays of his skull and then of his hand.

'Head is okay,' said the doctor, 'but there may be concussion. Fingers are okay too – badly sprained little finger, it'll hurt a bit. Pain-killers will help. Try not to use it. I know it will seem impossible, but try to avoid using it as much as you can.'

He turned to Sarah: 'I'd like to keep him in overnight, in case of concussion...'

'Oh, that won't be necessary, doctor,' she said. 'I'll stay with him tonight. I can recognise the symptoms of concussion. I'll bring him straight back if anything occurs.'

Shilling signed himself out.

Back in his hotel room there was no sign of the previous activity; her men had put everything back in its proper place. It looked as if they had even repaired the copier.

'Sorry about our date. Will you settle for room service? There's a menu on the table.'

'That's fine by me. But first, you get into bed. You're an invalid, remember.'

Shilling obediently stripped down to his boxer shorts and slid under the bed sheet. Every evening since arriving at the hotel he had put the duvet in the wardrobe and every morning it had been replaced on the bed by the housemaids.

Sarah sat on the bed and called room service with their choice of meal and of wine.

'So...' said Shilling: 'You were after the papyrus, too. I'd sort of sussed it out. You are in the reserve... you reported the information back home. They told you to get it. Luckily, you knew me well enough to chat me up, but they sent a couple of heavies in reserve. What were they supposed to do, to convince me?'

'It wasn't like that. Vanessa told you that I quite fancied you. That was true. I just hoped it might make things a little easier. The guys were for me, not for you – in case I needed any help, to run interference against anything from any other direction.'

'Well, what you're looking for is there, on the table beside the copier. It's a copy, like the one you saw at Profs' house on Saturday. I don't have the original.'

'But obviously, you know where it is.'

Shilling said he honestly didn't know.

'I'll tell you. When I realised how valuable it was I put it in a stiff backed envelope, then I put sheets of copier paper in nine other stiff-backed envelopes. Then I sealed them all, shuffled them so I didn't know which envelope contained the actual papyrus, and I addressed the envelopes to ten friends whose addresses I knew. Then I rang them and said they'd be getting an envelope with a Maltese stamp and would they please not open it, but save it for me until I collected it. When I get home I'll drive round and collect them. But I honestly don't know which of them will have the original.'

In the meantime, he told her, she could take a copy.

'If it's what I think it is – at least, the way Profs explains it – the copy is surely as useful as the original.'

'A copy is still only a copy... it depends on the proof of the original. We need to see it. We need to check it. Carbon dating and so on. And we need to know its whereabouts.'

'You only need proof if you think anybody might doubt it, or challenge its authenticity. When you say We, you mean... what... the Israeli government?'

'I suppose that's right, yes. I also mean the Jewish religion and the Jewish people.'

'...Who are your employers, at the end of the day?'

'Yes; who are my employers? I am still, as you say, a member of the military reserve.'

A waiter arrived with their meal. Using only his left hand Shilling ate from a tray, sitting up in the bed. Sarah took her plate to the table. She poured the wine and gave him half a glass.

'You mustn't drink too much, tonight.'

'I am thirsty. Excitement – adrenalin – builds up my thirst. It's only an hour or so ago that I watched you kill a man. And in my bedroom, too. I have to say that you appeared very efficient, and so did your back-up boys. Have you done much of that sort of thing before?'

'I have hit people, but never killed one. But, look... he was in the process of torturing you. I didn't come in until I heard you cry out. I don't think I'm going to lose much sleep over it.'

'What was it that you used – *Krav Maga*?'

Krav maga was a defensive – normally defensive – form of martial art that had been developed by the Israel Defence Force and by Mossad, the country's intelligence service. In Hebrew *Krav* means combat and *maga* means contact.

'Yes. Basically the blow to the side of the throat renders the victim unconscious; the middle of the forehead does much the same thing, but more reliably. It isn't necessarily a death-blow.'

'He worked for the Vatican. He was a priest of some sort. Does that make any difference?'

'No. There are good priests and bad priests, like any other profession. This one was torturing my friend: you. He was about to break a limb. I felt obliged to defend my friend. I didn't intend to kill him, only to stop him. But he died. It happens.'

Shilling thought it was probably how it had happened between Pace and McAuliffe. Pace hadn't intended to kill the man – he wanted only to extract information from him. He couldn't get it if the man was dead. But he had died. Yes; it happened. It happened even in his own experience; not in his personal experience, but in his colleagues'.

Police officers he'd worked with sometimes

overdid the aggression during interviews; it wasn't even necessarily physical, but some people couldn't take the strain of an over-intensive questioning. It could wreck a good copper's career.

The telephone interrupted his thoughts. It was Galea.

'While you've been out seeking pleasure, I have been in the office, working, and reading reports. And guess where Matey went today...?'

'*Ghidli.*' It was one of the few words of Maltese that Shilling had picked up. It was pronounced like *Idly*, and meant: *Tell me*.

'To visit the widow McAuliffe... Only, while knocking on the door he was spoken to by a local resident. When Pace went inside our man spoke to the passer-by and asked whether he knew him. He didn't. But he had seen him and spoken to him a week ago, last Monday night, when he was walking his dog...'

'Before putting it up on his roof to bark and annoy the neighbours...'

'Probably. But that puts him at the McAuliffe house at around eight o'clock. Enough, I'd say, to arrest him. What do you think?'

'Absolutely. This copper who spoke to the neighbour... was he on overtime?'

'I don't know; why do you ask?'

'I think you should put him down for a double shift. He's solved the case.'

'I thought I'd arrest him first thing in the morning. What do you think?'

'It's your call. Personally I don't like dawn raids.

Come round and have breakfast, here. Then we can go up in the lift leisurely and get him in his room. He's not going anywhere meanwhile.'

And that, thought Shilling, was certainly true: Pace had already taken his last journey.

What Shilling didn't say was that he now knew the motive for McAuliffe's murder. The Vatican was after the Jesus warrant.

How they knew about it, he had no idea except that he assumed they would know what treasures the Knights had possessed.

Nor had he any idea what had prompted them to come to Malta for it at this time.

Perhaps, he thought, there was some connection with the recent election of a new Pope.

Whatever it was, he was not going to share that bit of information with his Maltese colleague.

He replaced the telephone receiver, rolled over in the bed and fell asleep.

Five
It-Tlieta

When he woke his head was nestled between Sarah's naked and heavy breasts. It took a few seconds for him to remember how this had come about, and then to recall the events of the previous night.

He kissed her left breast, then nuzzled into her cleavage.

'You're awake, then. How's your head?'

'I think all my parts are working.'

'One of them certainly is.'

Man, woman, hotel room, king-size bed... There was no need for discussion; there was only one natural thing to do...

Sitting sipping coffee beside the window of the hotel dining room Shilling watched his Gozitan colleague arrive and speak to the two officers stationed outside in their car. As he came in Shilling stood and walked to the buffet and Galea joined him.

'Still in his room. As you said last night, there's no hurry.'

'How do they know he's in his room?'

'He was in it last night. He hasn't gone anywhere since.'

'Do they check, when they come on duty, that his car is in the car park?'

'I shouldn't think so. But it was there last night and nobody has seen it being driven out.'

Piling rashers of bacon onto his plate, Shilling asked: 'But couldn't he have driven out after the night shift went home last night?'

He thought he was behaving like a total shit, purposely deceiving a fellow police officer, but he was preparing Galea for the shock of finding their quarry gone.

'Why? There's nowhere for him to go. The ferry doesn't run all night, you know.'

They were served with fresh coffee and discussed their next steps in the case. Pace would be arrested 'on suspicion' in the first instance, then interviewed and almost certainly charged with the murder of John McAuliffe. They had a witness who could place him at the scene of the crime; hopefully his fingerprints would also match those on the whisky glass at the Gozo house and on the window pane at the Malta residence.

Case closed. Solved within a week.

'The only thing we still don't have,' said Shilling, 'is a motive.'

He knew Pace's motive only too well. There was no way, now, of Galea discovering it.

'He won't know that we don't know the motive. Hopefully it will come out, during the interview. He isn't going to know why we've – you've – arrested him.'

'Of course. That's got to be the way it happens. If he doesn't know that we don't know, he'll most likely drop it in to the conversation. It'll just come out naturally. What do you think it'll be?'

'No idea. We've discussed blackmail, bribery,

false claims for expenses from foreign governments. They are all possibilities. And we still can't rule out simple robbery. Maybe the guy stole something that hasn't been missed yet.'

Shilling said he thought that was unlikely. 'Why would he still be here, if that was the case? Why would he have gone back to the house if he had already taken whatever it was he wanted?'

'They always return to the scene of the crime. Anyway, let's go and pick up Matey.'

'Chummy,' said Shilling.

There was no answer when Galea knocked on the door of Pace's room so he showed his warrant card to a housemaid who was trundling her trolley along the corridor and she opened it for them.

The room was empty. So were the wardrobe and the chest of drawers. There was no sign that the room had been recently occupied. Sarah's boys had done a very thorough job, thought Shilling.

'Car park.'

They took the lift to the basement: no sign of the silver Escort. Galea ran up the ramp to the officers on duty outside. No; they said; they hadn't seen the car leave – if it had left they would be following it, wouldn't they?

'You have the car details, Put out a call for it. All parts of the island, and the other side, too. He might be on the ferry. Or he might have been on the ferry, maybe first crossing this morning. That would be five o'clock. And check returned hire cars at the airport. What time did you come on duty?'

'Seven, *Sur*-inspector; that's the time we were told to start.'

'Shit! Shit! Shit!'

'Relax,' Shilling told him. 'Like you said earlier, there's nowhere to go. How far away could he possibly be? Let's go and finish our coffee...'

The waitress brought them a fresh pot and they sat drinking in depressed silence.

Galea stared at Shilling, filled with curiosity. The man from Scotland Yard had actually asked whether his officers had checked that the car was in the car park when they had come on duty. They should have done that. He had even said it was possible that Pace had driven out after the night shift had gone home. He must have some sort of second sight, he decided; a useful attribute for a police officer.

Shilling was topping up their cups when one of the cops came rushing in.

'*Sur inspekter*...! Come quickly! They have found the car!'

The senior officers rose quickly from the table.

Shilling patted Galea on the back as they headed for the door. 'Bloody marvellous. Bloody quick, too. What did I tell you...?'

The police driver passed Galea a microphone through the car window and he spoke rapidly to the operations room. He grabbed Shilling's elbow and steered him towards his own car.

'Come on! We've found the car. They are lifting it out of the sea, down in the harbour, right now!'

Pace's silver Escort was hanging from a ten-wheel mobile crane when the two police cars arrived at the jetty, just beyond the ferry terminal. Broad canvas straps were attached to each wheel and water poured out of the door sills, back into the sea. There were two police divers in the water beneath it.

Galea spoke to the sergeant from the police station at the harbour. There were no visible brake marks or skid marks on the concrete jetty, he was told.

They waited and watched until the flow of water reduced to a dribble, then the crane swung the car round and lowered it gently to the ground. Officers opened each of the front doors, stepping back quickly as more sea water emptied from the car's interior.

A police photographer recorded each stage of the procedure, finally moving closer to take pictures of the sole occupant from either side, through each of the open front doors.

Galea and Shilling moved forward for a closer look.

'That's your man,' said Shilling.

An ambulance arrived and the paramedics waited while a police doctor made a cursory examination of the body and pulled the seat belt so that it sprang slowly and soggily back into the central column. More photographs were taken before the lifeless form of Loretto Pace was transferred to a trolley and then into the ambulance.

'Looks like a straightforward drowning,' the doctor told Galea.

'But I can't be sure until the autopsy.'

'Quick as you can, please. He's the major suspect in a murder case.'

The doctor checked his watch. 'Come and see me at lunchtime.'

Galea told one of the officers to open the boot. He needed the keys for this and Shilling caught the man's arm and told him: 'Before you remove the keys from the dashboard, check whether the ignition was on or off.'

The ignition was on, the constable told him. He opened the boot and it was full of water and contained a suitcase.

'Leave it,' said Galea. 'We can open it at headquarters.'

They stood about, with nothing to do until a low loader arrived and the crane lifted the car on to it. Then they followed the vehicle on its slow journey to the police garage.

Galea phoned magistrate Scicluna to brief him on details of the sudden death and its assumed relationship to the McAuliffe inquiry.

The magistrate said he would organise an independent forensic investigation of the harbour incident. He also congratulated the officer on what appeared to be a solution to the murder case.

Shilling then followed Galea into the superintendent's office.

It was sparsely furnished and Shilling noticed a camp bed and a hanging locker in an alcove at the side of the room. It made sense: the senior officer would not work regular hours, so if he found time to snatch a siesta in the heat of the day or worked through the night a camp bed would be handy.

Galea started making his report in Maltese but his boss nodded then pointed in Shilling's direction and he switched comfortably into English for the benefit of their visitor.

'...So...' he concluded, 'We are just waiting to tie up some loose ends, but I am pretty confident that we have cracked it.'

'It looks like, between the two of you, you've solved one suspicious death and found yourselves another,' the superintendent told them.

'Solved a murder, and now looking into an accidental death,' said Galea.

'Ah,' said Shilling... 'The accidental death's not my problem. My work here is done. I'll probably go back tomorrow.'

True to his promise the pathologist had a preliminary report when they called on him at lunchtime.

'It's not conclusive, I'm afraid. There was some water, but not a lot, in his lungs, so whatever it is I'd say that drowning was not the primary cause of death. Time of death... it's difficult to be precise because the sea water is a different temperature from the air temperature, but somewhere between about nine o'clock and midnight. There's a slight mark on the right side of his neck: an abrasion rather than a bruise...'

'Seat belt?' asked Galea.

'Quite possibly, yes. And there's another mark on the forehead. But something stopped the heart pumping blood around the body, leading to cardiac arrest. The seat belt wasn't fastened properly; he could have hit his head on the steering wheel. Nothing to suggest the involvement of drink or drugs. It could be a culmination of events – seat belt, as you say... car hitting the water, and water is harder when you hit it than most people would expect... possibly his head hitting the steering wheel – you can do that, of course, even while wearing a seat belt, if you move forward gradually. But he could have been dead before he entered the water.'

'So the cause of death...?'

'Well, basically, a heart stoppage. Some form of heart attack. I can't really be more specific.'

'So,' said Shilling, 'if he had a heart attack when driving towards the edge of the pier, maybe lost consciousness and the car kept moving forward...'

'There is nothing to stop that happening,' Galea told the doctor. 'There are no railings where the car went in. It's where the fishermen sit.'

'That wouldn't have caused a mark from the seat belt,' said the doctor.

'It's more likely that he went off the edge accidentally, in the dark. Handbrake wasn't applied. Seat belt jarred the side of his neck... he could have hit the steering wheel... then the car hits the water... I would think that would create a series of shocks to the system... Then heart failure.'

'Then the actual death would be natural causes, if he died on the jetty.'

'Or accidental death, anyway, if he died as a result of driving off it.'

'Either way, that's not my problem. It's just something for the coroner to decide: accidental death or natural causes. And almost certainly not death by drowning. But it isn't murder, then. And not suicide. That's the important thing...'

'It would have been the most inefficient way to attempt suicide, said the doctor. 'He wouldn't have died until his lungs filled with water and he drowned. No reason for me to suspect murder, although, if he had been killed somehow and then his car driven off the jetty...'

'Let's not even go there. One way or another it was quite clearly an accident, eh?'

'That's my first impression from my preliminary findings. Of course, further investigation may produce some other cause.'

'What's the point of that?' Galea asked him. 'It's not going to make any difference to the widow...'

'There's no widow,' Shilling reminded him.

'The man's a priest.'

'That's it, then. And if there is any insurance involvement, the way he died won't make any difference to them.'

'One other thing,' said the doctor as the policemen made for the door.' Your fingerprint people were here. They said there was an involvement with another case...'

'That's what we are hoping for,' said Shilling, as the rubber door swung shut behind them.

guess, if you are parking between the lamps and in the shadows.'

'We still don't know how he managed to get out of the hotel, though.'

'I can help you there. You invited the detectives inside the hotel for a drink. He would have left at that time; I'd say that's fairly obvious.'

'As far as we know, though, he had no idea that he was being followed. Surely he wouldn't have gone back to the McAuliffe house if he'd known we were following him.'

'Except that there was still something that he wanted at the house, or at one of the houses, and he would be making a last effort to get it. I've checked, and Mrs McAuliffe says she didn't give him anything except a drink, and as far as she knows he didn't take anything, and he didn't find the safe...'

'Fairly obviously he didn't find it, because the safe was at the other house, in Birgu.'

'Correct. Maybe she said something to him, though, about our enquiries. Anyway, he was making his getaway, late last night. Late because he was waiting to leave in darkness.'

'Empty handed...'

'Well, we have found nothing on his person or in his car or suitcase that looks as if it was stolen from the McAuliffes. So, yes: empty-handed.'

'What you are saying, or implying, then, is that what has happened is all my fault.'

Shilling was content to take the blame. Galea had either forgotten about the piece of papyrus or thought it was of no consequence; he was relieved about that. And even if he'd known that Mrs McAuliffe had told Pace about the von Hompesch portrait, Galea would have written it off as being a most unlikely object of anybody's desire.

He was still annoyingly aware that he was behaving in a totally deceitful manner with a fellow copper.

But he needed to test the theory.

'We have Pace – Chummy – at the scene of the crime, in fact at the scenes of two crimes. We also have a witness to establish the timing of his presence to coincide with the murder. What we still don't have is a motive.'

'Oh, I'm not worried about that. McAuliffe was shifting money about, to and from the Vatican Bank, and there's also his link with the Freemasons, that he admitted to you. That's the beauty of it. We have solved the murder and we can hand the papers over to the Fraud Squad and they can investigate the movement of money and perhaps they will come up with a motive. But as far as we are concerned, the murder is solved. That was our job: the murder, not the motive.'

'But I screwed things up, you think?'

Shilling hung his head in a pretence of shame.

'Not at all, Bob. If you did inadvertently let anything slip, it caused his flight because he feared being arrested. If I'd arrested him I would need to get a confession or at least a motive out of him, then there'd be all the complications of banks and banking and involvement with the Masons and – worse – diplomatic complications with the Vatican.

My suspicion is that it is all connected to the Vatican Bank. There was a case in London, in the eighties...'

'I know. In fact my father worked on it. It came to nothing.'

'My Super wouldn't have fancied any of that. The guys in Malta can worry about it now. We don't have a fraud squad this side of the Channel.'

'No fraud on Gozo, eh?'

'Only the fairly blatant type; not usually too difficult to detect.'

'So you've solved a murder in a week, or thereabouts, and I can go home.'

'Not *I* have solved it, Bob; *we* have solved it together. You have been a great help. And you also picked up that other information for your people back home that isn't related to any criminal activity involving Malta.'

'Except for Malta being the route that most of the stuff was shipped out on from Libya.'

'Apart from that; yes. I'll get my boss to talk to somebody, maybe the Commissioner, about tightening things up in relation to that sort of thing.

'It wouldn't be a bad idea.'

AFTERMATH

'Was it really necessary to erase McAuliffe?'

Alasdair Lamont had parked his car – against the rules – on the road than ran through the golf course at Moor Park, just north of London. He had stepped on to the grass, realised that it was still wet from the previous day's rain, then taken a pair of rubber over-shoes from the boot of his car and pulled them on. He walked across onto the close-cropped turf of a green where Leo Dillon was practising his putting.

With the ratio of one CCTV camera for every fourteen people in England it was difficult to find a place where you could meet unobserved, but golf courses were generally a safe bet.

'Erased...? is that the latest euphemism? You no longer use eliminated, or terminated with extreme prejudice?'

'Erased: rubbed out; wiped out... It sounds much less aggressive, don't you think?'

'Whatever. You should ask the erasers – is that the expression you'd use? – and that would be the Holy Romans.'

'It wasn't your lot?'

'We didn't arrive there until two days later. He was... erased on the Monday; our man arrived on the Wednesday.'

Lamont looked down at his ankles and saw that his trousers turn-ups were soaking wet.

'But you have people there, don't you, *in situ*?'

'You know we don't. We operate only on home turf. Abroad is your exclusive domain.'

'That's not strictly true, though, is it? I mean, your man Shilling has worked abroad before... Germany...'

'You've had his file out? In any case, that was Berlin. British sector.'

'Austria doesn't have a British sector.'

'Used to. But that was post mortem, invited in by the locals, same as this one.'

'Canada...'

'Part of the British Commonwealth.'

'As is Malta.'

'But we don't have representatives there. Unlike you. Malta would obviously be the perfect listening post for Libya.'

'So you're saying you didn't do it? I just thought there might have been easier ways of extracting the information.'

'I am not just saying that we didn't do it. We didn't do it, full stop. And there obviously wasn't an easier way, because he wouldn't part with the information to the Romans. It's all in Shilling's report.'

'And he didn't do it?'

'He wasn't on the island, and nor was anybody else from my lot. The guy who did it confessed to Shilling.'

'Then Shilling bumped... erased... him?'

'No. You can blame that one on the Jews.'

'Anyway, he did a good job. You should tell him.'

'I have done.'

'You been following the Maltese rags?'

'I haven't; Shilling has.'

'Interesting that the McAuliffe inquest came up so quickly. Miraculous speed for the Malts. And then it was simply person or persons unknown.'

'Shilling said it was so they could press on with the funeral; he said there are hundreds of bodies in the mortuary, just waiting for a coroner, but the McAuliffes have money.'

'Then this Maltese priest, who may or may not be connected to the Vatican bank, on holiday from Rome, drives himself off the jetty. Another indecently hasty inquest: accidental death this time, with a warning from the coroner to check your seat belt and your handbrake.'

'The guy worked for the Vatican. The Maltese wouldn't want them to think they were being messed about.'

'And finally it's leaked, from Malta, that the local police and Scotland Yard suspect a connection between the death of McAuliffe and the Vatican Bank.'

'I know; Shilling leaked it. Apparently he has contacts on the island. It made an effective smoke-screen for the arms-dealing stuff.'

'I know who leaked it. So there's a funny thing: you have nobody in Malta, but Shilling just happens to know somebody, eh?'

'Friend of his father's, it turns out.'

'Of course. Yes... it would be. And God's Nazi has already announced that the Vatican intends to hold an inquiry into the banking.'

Lamont walked back to his car with his hands in

his pockets, holding the cuffs of his trousers above the height of the cut grass.

The *Apostolic Nuncio*, the Pope's ambassador to Great Britain, lives and works in the Vatican's embassy overlooking Wimbledon Common in south-west London. And it was there that Bob Shilling was invited for lunch on his first day off work after returning to Scotland Yard.

The door was opened for him by the *Nuncio*'s chaplain, a monsignor, who led him into a drawing room and asked him to wait. He had sat there alone for ten minutes and was looking around the room for an ashtray when a tall figure in cardinal's cassock entered with the chaplain who introduced them and left.

'So... Inspector Shilling... Now that you're here, what do you want?'

'Well...' Shilling couldn't bring himself to use the correct form of address, which he knew would be Your Eminence. He was not a Catholic and the title sounded to him quite ludicrous, out-dated since the days of Cardinal Richelieu... 'You invited me...'

'Exactly. So... what do you want?'

'I'm not sure what you mean.'

'I mean do you want sweet or dry?'

'Oh... dry, please.'

'Excellent.' And the cardinal crossed the room to a cocktail cabinet and began mixing a cocktail that seemed to involve a number of colourless spirits.

He handed a glass to Shilling, then raised his own.

'Salute.'

Shilling responded with 'Good health.'

It tasted wonderful on the tongue and provided a kick when it reached the back of the throat. Shilling thought he might ask, later, for the recipe.

'Very good. Very dry,' he said, raising his glass again, this time in appreciation. 'So... what do *you* want?'

The cardinal shook his head with a slight shrug. That could come later.

'The chaplain should have asked, when he telephoned. Is there anything you don't eat, or prefer not to eat? Are you familiar with, and do you have any objection to, *ossobuco*?'

'Yes and no,' Shilling told him; 'I love it.'

He was asked what he thought of Malta, whether it had been his first visit, what he thought of the people, and told that he had retained a slight but healthy looking tan. It occurred to Shilling that business would be postponed until the meal was over: the Mediterranean way – food first, business second.

The cross-cut veal shanks were so tender Shilling barely needed to use his knife which was good because his little finger still hurt. They were the best he'd ever tasted. When the chaplain brought in coffee he sat and joined them at the large table.

'You know of course why I asked to see you,' he said.

Shilling said nothing.

The cardinal said nothing until their cups were refilled.

'A *digestivo*, perhaps?'

'No thanks.'

There was another long silence. Then the cardinal spoke again and said that he would – of course – be more than happy to pay a sum of money to Shilling as compensation for the trouble he had gone to in acquiring and safeguarding the article in question. A very large amount of money, he said.

'I suppose you would. After all, you were prepared to kill for it.'

The cardinal may have been sincerely apologetic but it was difficult for Shilling to interpret his facial expression.

'A tragedy,' he said. 'An accident with the worst possible consequences. Perhaps it was just a slightly over-enthusiastic handling of the situation.'

'Nevertheless, a man died. Tell me, does *Thou shalt not kill* mean nothing to your people? Or what about *Thou shalt not steal*? Because your man was clearly planning to steal it, if he couldn't get his hands on it in any other way. I suppose there is no Commandment to say thou shalt not torture – there couldn't be, could there – to the people who invented the Inquisition?'

People didn't talk like that to cardinals. But the cleric remained cool. Money, he knew, could often have a calming effect on anger.

'The figure we had in mind was something equivalent to one million pounds, sterling.'

'You don't get it, do you?' Shilling sounded angry; his harsh interrogator's voice... 'Your man Pace tortured and killed a British businessman while working under orders from the Vatican. You simply cannot escape involvement in that man's death. He was working for you!'

The cardinal clearly had not been kept fully in the picture about Pace's quest, and he obviously could know nothing about the final stage of his venture.

'And then... still working under orders and presumably under the supervision of the Vatican, he attempted to torture me! Given what happened to the tragic Mr McAuliffe, it seems safe to assume that he was equally prepared to kill me, to satisfy you!'

'I – we – knew nothing about that.'

'I don't suppose you did. But torturing a police officer doesn't go down well with the courts in Britain, nor even in Malta. And, before he died, Pace told me everything. It's all in my notebook.'

That was a lie. Shilling had not made notes about his final conversation with Pace because policemen's notebooks could always be read by their superior officers and there were some things that he didn't want anybody to know. But the conversation he'd had with Pace was indelibly etched into his memory; it could be entered into the book at any time.

'I also have this friend, an English journalist. He's a freelance now, and works for all the papers. He'd just love a story about a Vatican secret, a murder conspiracy, and torture and murder. Murder in the furtherance of theft... it used to be a hanging matter, you know.'

The cardinal bit his lower lip.

'I think we might be able to stretch to two million. That would of course be tax free, and payable discreetly in the currency of your choice into any bank that you named, anywhere in the world.'

'You do a lot of this... negotiating, do you?'

'No, I don't.'

'I didn't think so.' Shilling thought the time was right to use the title: 'Well, *your eminence*, you can go whistle. It isn't for sale. Certainly not to you, anyway.'

'Are you planning to offer it to a buyer elsewhere? Whoever that was, we would be prepared to offer more.'

'You're referring to the Jews, I suppose. The people you have been slandering for two millennia...'

Shilling shrugged, as if the discussion was of little importance to him.

'Tell you what... make it five million, and I won't give the original document to the Jews.'

The cardinal appeared to be unfazed by the amount of money.

'Are you serious?'

'Deadly.'

'I would need to take advice.'

'Take it. Then give me a call, over the weekend. I'm like you: for me, Sunday is a working day.'

Shilling returned to central London and then took a taxi to Palace Green in Kensington. The Israeli embassy had once been the home of William Makepiece Thackeray, author of *Vanity Fair*, and then a Montessori school before being bought by the Tel Aviv government.

He was aware of CCTV cameras following him along the garden path, then of being photographed from every angle as he stood at the door and announced his name and the fact that he had an appointment. The door opened automatically and he found himself confronted by a box, half glass and half concrete-reinforced steel, about the size of a hotel lift. He repeated his identity and details of his appointment and presented his warrant card to the lens of yet another camera. The heavy six-inch thick door swung smoothly open and he stepped inside the embassy and found the ambassador, a man that he knew, waiting to greet him.

They exchanged courtesies and he was led to a drawing room where another man, a stranger this time, stood to greet him.

'Dr *Field*...? So...'

'You have already met my daughter, I know.'

They were served with coffee and left alone to talk.

They made small talk; Shilling was fully familiar by now with the Mediterranean way.

Finally, Dr Field said: 'So, you have this...'

Papyrus, document, paper, warrant, artefact, even treasure: it had been described in many different ways. Dr Field didn't give it a name. They both knew what he was talking about.

'And now you want to sell it.'

'Do I?'

'I think so. But we don't want to buy it. You gave Sarah a photocopy of it and that is sufficient for us. We knew that it existed, or we believed that it existed. The copy is sufficient for our needs. We may need to use it, or at least refer to its existence, at some time in the future. If we had the original, it would require carbon-dating, first, then poring over for years by experts. So we don't need it. On the other hand, we are rather concerned about the possibility of other people destroying the original.'

'That's not going to happen.'

'You think that Rome will lodge it in their secret archive and preserve it for posterity? And not – given the implications of its very existence – destroy it?'

'They offered to buy it. I told them it's not for sale.'

'So it's available for sale to us, you mean?'

'Obviously not, since you don't want to buy it.'

'We don't want it, but we don't want it to be destroyed. You can no doubt keep it safe somewhere for the rest of your lifetime, but what happens then? This thing is already two thousand years old; it is timeless.'

Shilling said that he had made arrangements for the safekeeping of the papyrus for eternity – 'or what we currently understand to be meant by eternity'.

'I would feel a lot more comfortable if you could explain that to me.'

Shilling could, and did. Before leaving Gozo and taking the ferry to Malta and the flight back to England he had called on Professor Ashe and told him about the dilemma of being in possession of a priceless artefact but not knowing what to do with it, nor who were the rightful owners of it.

Ashe said there was no rightful owner. If Scotland Yard issued a wanted poster, it would not be their property once they had handed it to a member of the public, or hung it in a pub or pasted it on a wall. The writing of it would be their copyright, but there was no copyright law in the first century. The Roman Empire had, in theory, created the document but that empire no longer existed; it was too easy, and a falsehood, he said, to assume that the Holy Roman Empire was the natural successor of the Caesars.

'As I understand the situation,' he told Shilling, 'you are content for people to know that it exists, and maybe even to see it under secure conditions. But you don't want anybody to physically get their hands on it.'

'Plus the fact that it is incredibly fragile. It might not actually last very long in any case.'

'There is one place. There is an archive that I think would be appropriate. It is an archive that is far more secret than, for example, the Vatican's own so-called secret archive.'

'More secret?'

'So secret that nobody knows about it. Well... that is... nobody except a very small and select number of English historians, of which I am privileged to be one. Quite simply, it is sometimes important for historians to know how things happen or why they had happened in order to maintain the accuracy of English history; but without revealing the full details or the source of knowledge.'

Shilling said he understood that. But now that he knew the secret of the existence of the archives, if he agreed to lodge the warrant inside it for safe keeping – possibly for eternity – how much about its whereabouts could he reveal?

To anybody who was likely to handle the information with discretion, Ashe told him, he could repeat as much as he knew himself.

'The thing is... there'll be quite a few people who won't believe it in any case.'

Shilling spent his next annual holiday in Israel with Sarah Field.

He had told nobody that the flight and accommodation were being paid for by the Israeli government. It would have been against the code of conduct for a police officer to accept such an offer but he didn't care because he had already written his resignation from the Metropolitan Police.

Sarah and her father took him to the Knesset where he was introduced to the president and then presented with the President's Medal which it was explained to him was awarded to people 'who have made an outstanding contribution to the State of Israel or to humanity, through their talents, services, or in any other form.'

'As I understand the situation,' Dr Field told him, smiling, 'you will not be able to wear this without permission from Queen Elizabeth. If you think it would help, I could write to her.'

Shilling, who did not intend to wear a uniform ever again, thanked him and said it wouldn't be necessary.

After lunch Sarah drove him to Jerusalem and

showed him the streets and buildings associated with the life of Christ. 'They don't fit the story,' Shilling told her, astonished. 'It couldn't possibly have been like that!'

'Of course it couldn't,' she agreed.

'But it isn't about history: it's about faith.'

In early February 2013 speaking in Latin at the Apostolic Palace in the *Sala del Concistoro*, and citing his deteriorating strength through old age, Pope Benedict XVI announced that, after fewer than eight years in the job he intended to resign. He would be the first Pope not to die in office since the curia had sacked the 'Vicar of Christ' six hundred years earlier.

One month later, in what was described as a surprise result, Jorge Mario Bergoglio of Argentina who had been Cardinal Ratzinger's rival for the position in 2005 was elected to succeed him.

According to the Vatican news agency, when he addressed the College of Cardinals for the first time as Pope Francis, he surveyed the array of red robes and, looking at none of them directly, said:

'May God forgive you all.'

#

THE HITLER SCOOP

Revel Barker's debut novel (also available in e-book form as *Hitler: The Last Conspiracy*) was described by the *Northern Echo* as 'the most thought-provoking book of the year' and chosen by the *Yorkshire Post* as its Book Of The Month. The *Daily Mail* said it was 'full of Arthur Daley-type characters'.

Deeply researched and based partly on the diaries of Dr Theo Morell, Hitler's personal physician in the Berlin Bunker, it includes a factual account of conflicting reports of the Führer's last days in Germany – plus recently revealed DNA evidence about the remains that the Soviet Union claimed to belong to Hitler.

THE MAYOR OF MONTEBELLO

The writing of this chart-topping political novel (also available in e-book format) was compared by professional reviewers with the works of P G Wodehouse, Compton McKenzie and *Don Camillo* author Giovannino Guareschi.

Diplomat magazine described it as 'hugely funny'.

The book chronicles the first year in office of an Englishman who accidentally, and against his will, finds himself elected mayor of a remote Sicilian island. The island is crime-free – except for the occasional necessary murder.

P

Palatino Publishing

palatinobooks@gmail.com

www.ingramcontent.com/pod-product-compliance
Ingram Content Group UK Ltd.
Pitfield, Milton Keynes, MK11 3LW, UK
UKHW020224250726
13967UKWH00001B/183

9 781907 841118